GUARDIANS 2

JOHN GUTHRIE

My thanks to Robert Harrison of Seneca Author Services for his formatting,
cover design and invaluable assistance with everything even slightly technical.

Paperback ISBN: 978-1-0684612-0-0

For Michael,
for persuading me to do it.

FOREWORD

Every tyranny stands on a firm foundation of petty bureaucracy.

— THE PROFESSOR

PROLOGUE

"THE BIGGEST PROBLEM," said the Professor, "apart from your need to avoid detection, is to reach a point of certainty about a potential recruit at a safe distance of time before the enemy does."

"Assuming the enemy will wait to become certain."

"Yes. On that point, I am counting on their constant desire to do things by procedures and verify everything before acting on evidence. But the problem within the problem is that you will be drawing your potential recruit on, tempting into bigger misdemeanours. And if the person is caught, there must be no rescue. At least, not until the right time. Clear?"

"Yes."

I said it with deliberate firmness. I'd already been rejected and admonished several times for displaying very slight hesitation in my responses. But the Professor was right. He had done his part perfectly, creating the person that I was going to become. Now, it was up to me to *be* that person. Not *act* that person: *be* that person. A thoroughly indoctrinated, callous school student, during which I had to endure constant surveillance and risk arrest and punishment. In attempting to destroy the system, I had to become one of its efficient and eager little monsters.

"Do you think you are ready?"

I looked at that intense face, always expressing compassion and ruthlessness, spirituality and pragmatism, astonishing intelligence and trusting innocence. The man who had been training me for two years; who had driven me beyond the limits of endurance; who had broken and dismantled me, then constructed a different me.

I waited for him to remove the straps which bound my ankles and wrists, so familiar to me after the many times that he had conducted mock tortures, with varying amounts of real pain.

Two years of being broken and reconstructed, of being reassembled, of being replaced by this new person that I was to be, Javid Yong, Citizen Student, while retaining in a secret place in my mind, my real identity.

Whoever and whatever that was now.

The fear of detection was not my only fear: I was afraid of this new person. So far, I had acted through the many sessions. Out there, down there, there would be no acting. That was the horror, the dread. Could I return to being me? Would I become what those others had become, or always been?

I glanced up at the little black disc which hovered nearby. My little protector from them, and, I hoped, from myself. My own precious guardian.

"I'm ready," I said. "Untie me and let me go to it."

"It isn't quite time," he said, with a slight shadow passing over that face which I knew so well. "It wasn't a problem before that hair must be short, and no facial hair is permitted. Hiding the face, they call it. So, with no whiskering to hide your boyish looks, I must do something else."

I tried to take a deep breath, but my chest felt suddenly heavy. "What is it?" I asked, starting to tremble in spite of the tight bonds round my wrists.

"I've changed you inside," he said softly. "Now, I'm going to change you outside." He smiled with emotion. "Your voice has been lowered and made harsh. I have worked on your skin with sandpaper and rough plants. But you still look like Lanny. I'm going to make you look like Javid."

I felt the slight prick of the needle in my neck. Close to tears, determined to be callous even to myself, I said, "I don't want to know what you're going to do."

The words crawled out through a mouth which was already becoming numb.

He nodded his agreement.

His fist crushed my nose.

CHAPTER ONE

ON A FINE, sunny day, I stood at the edge of State Park 49, trying not to look at a hovering disc. Even when they weren't watching you, they were watching you. I was a human being, and a Citizen 3. A Citizen Student. So I was watched. It could detect my status through the location chip in my thumb, and the IG in my head. At least, I hoped it could. The Professor had made and inserted mine.

The discs were everywhere now. They had replaced birds as the constant flying things above our heads and all around us. A favourite manoeuvre was to drop down and hover right in front of you, giving the impression that they were staring at you, into you, knowing all your secrets.

Since even standing still could make a disc or an OG suspicious, I set off across the Park.

To my left, two other discs were moving quickly, away. I wondered what emergency had sent them hurrying. What had someone done, or said? With the slightest turn of my head, I was relieved to see the other one sliding away through the air.

What else had changed while I had been away? The existence of a hierarchy was now clearly displayed, with a team of twelve supported by a new executive level, with gold badges on their blue uniforms. And above the team of twelve, there were a Citizen President and a Citizen Prime Minister. Large posters with their photographs were on many walls. Inevitably, they looked like ordinary, amiable people.

There were regular group confessions, rectifications, atonements. Citizen 2's who had done things which a committee decided was against the State could be demoted, wearing a brown sash over their uniforms.

Hats were so precisely measured to ensure that there was no covering or even shading of the face, that they had virtually disappeared. In a tyranny, instead of forbidding everything, you could merely make it so that people decided that this or that wasn't worth the risk or the bother. No need to ban the wearing of hats: just impose a punishment for a brim which was a hair's breadth past the limit, and let people place the actual restriction on themselves.

Children were playing in the Park. They were playing the only permitted game: the State against the Capitalists. The State soldiers must always win, and the Capitalists must always be captured, harangued and shot. No-one wanted to be the Capitalists, so there was always a minor game within the game to choose whose turn it was.

This wasn't the shortest route to school, which made it a risk. But I hadn't spoken to Katina for a couple of days, and there were still some small trees in the Park where she could hide.

I walked slowly by a Japanese Maple tree, trying hard not to look suspicious, which always looked suspicious. I counted six discs looping around nearby.

"Those things make it difficult," said Katina from a low branch.

"Things have changed more than the Professor could find in the computer system. These things, for one. And this calling everyone 'Citizen'. It's driving me mad."

"Don't let it. You have a job to do. Focus. Be absorbed into how things *are*, not how they *were*. Don't let yourself out."

"Thank you for the lecture. I'd better start moving again. This is not the direct route to school."

There was no response, and I assumed she'd gone. That was okay. She was sticking to the script, and I wasn't. When you are focused on the task, you accept things as they are, and you certainly don't let them drive you mad.

The school assembly yard resembled a funeral gathering. Children walked slowly, silently about, or stood silently still. When someone did speak, the voice penetrated the silence like a stone thrown in stagnant water.

"Citizen Student Hollis. You performed well in last night's gym."

"I have practised hard, Citizen Student O'Tate."

No greetings were exchanged, or even acknowledgments of one's presence. I assumed my aloof expression, and joined the slow walkers until the bell rang and we entered the building.

My thumb chip gave a tiny beep as I walked through the beam, which was always a relief.

The day began in our assembly class. As always, we were all there. No-one was ill because we all took the mandatory anti-everything pills. With no other causes for absence, we received the customary State command to be loyal to the State in everything we did, big or small and went straight to the first lesson.

The only good thing in the State education system was that the State's only interest was in my absorbing false history and propaganda. And that made it easy. So long as I could recite any of that on demand, then the State was satisfied. It had no interest in my absorbing true facts about anything. There were occasional tests, but there was no response after the papers were collected by the teacher. So, I could concentrate on playing my role without being distracted by having to acquire a lot of mundane stuff. The teacher threw the education ball, and I caught it and threw it back to him.

This emptying yourself of all curiosity and interest could be done with surprising simplicity and ease. The difficult part was retaining that tiny capsule of *me* in its hidden place, deep within my mind.

"Citizen Yong!" Citizen Teacher Shaw was looking at me. "You daydream. You are bored?"

I stood and looked repentant. "No, Citizen Teacher. I was thinking of uses of the beautiful knowledge in this lesson."

"I tell you to think of uses?"

"No, Citizen Teacher."

"Then stop it!"

I didn't say, 'Yes, Citizen Teacher'. That was called 'last-wording'. The teacher must be the last one to speak. I indicated my humility and remorse by bowing my head, then slowly sitting down.

This aspect of school was much worse now. Obedience and submission must be constantly displayed. I was having to learn all the changes rapidly. I couldn't make the excuse that I didn't know; but that meant I had deliberately disobeyed. There must be no errors.

I stared at Citizen Teacher Shaw as she related a garbled history of the State. In this history, the State had existed for thousands of years, but over all that time, it had been fighting a bitter battle against Capitalist Right-Wingers, who were super-stitious fiends, worshipping mythical beasts, invading, enslaving, stealing. And on and on, until the glorious present, when the State had thrown off the yoke of oppression, fought back, and WON.

I had learned that the State had thrown off the yoke of oppression all over the world. It had entered and overthrown country after country, defending itself. It was called 'anticipatory counterattack'.

I knew all this because the Professor had given me history lessons, and let me read books. Real, old books. I learned about the different countries, and their long histories. Oppression and domination went in cycles. Countries gave the world great learn-ing, then fell back into ignorance. Sometimes, it was the progression from greatness into decadence; often, this or that religion claimed, insisted, that it would do all the necessary thinking. Then, when the people had stopped thinking, they did everything that they were told to do, and believed everything that they were told to believe.

Startled, I asked the Professor, "Isn't that like the State now?"

He replied, "Yes, Lanny. It's just a different sort of religion. Religion should be concerned only with the exploration and development of spiritual matters, not the control of people."

The Professor told me about real history, and about many other things that he knew. And he told me about a lot of things that he didn't know. He didn't make things up to fill in the gaps, or to cover up bits that he didn't like.

"Now this," he said, "is one of the most important things. In telling lies about almost everything, the State is like many people who are compulsive liars. In the same way, the State tells lies when, even from its own perspective, there is no need. But this comes from the necessary habit of telling lies to follow every other lie. When you lie about something which happened in history, then you have to tell another lie about what happened after the thing that happened, and another lie after that. And the further back the event which is first being lied about, the longer the trail of necessary lies to account for what happened after the first event."

"Citizen Student Yong!"

I stood. "Yes, Citizen Teacher."

How long had it taken for those thoughts to pass through my mind in a brief remembering? Long enough for her to detect my lack of interest. That was careless. I had slipped out of my role, again. I was like someone who trains in a gymnasium with heavy weights, but can't resist frequently touching his biceps to feel his progress. In the classroom, I must be entirely a willing student of the propaganda. It was not the time or place for ponderings.

"Citizen Student, I told you a few minutes ago to stop daydreaming. You just did it again."

"Citizen Teacher. I humbly regret my error. Your lectures inspire and stimulate. I try to think of ways to be worthy of them."

I spoke in the brightly mechanical way of an exemplary student. I knew that the words and the delivery had an ingenuous power. "Not in class," she said firmly, but without the nerve-shredding sharpness. "Wait until after."

I bowed so low that my head almost hit the desk. I stopped thinking, stared and concentrated. The constant requirement was to concentrate, focus, absorb. It was inevitable that much of it stuck in the brain. But it must be stuck in mine like food which sticks in the teeth, to be disposed of as soon as possible.

Stop thinking! Listen and absorb.

CHAPTER TWO

THE TARGET WAS MIKEL BROVNIK. There were subtle, slight signs. An occasional sigh, almost a smile. The little things which might indicate a suitable person. I had observed and reported, and the Professor had told me to work on it. He had looked at Mikel's background, so far as it was recorded in the central records. There was little to see. That was good. I wanted to see the signs, but I didn't want others to see them.

This was the weekly lecture, in the Big Hall, the whole school required to attend. He was sitting in the middle of the audience. That wasn't the best position. That was what people did when they wanted to be anonymous, when they were afraid of being easily available for scrutiny. Little things were so important. There was nowhere to hide. Outside and inside, they watched you. With cameras and microphones, with implants and chips, with OGs and discs, and with everyone else, watching and listening, eager to report you. Don't draw attention to yourself, but don't try to be inconspicuous.

And be a constant, tittle-tattling, gossiping sneak.

The more you denounced, or reported, or suggested, the safer you were.

Until it was your turn. Until the finger pointed at you. But until then, you watched, listened, and told; watched, listened, and told.

When such thoughts appeared, I immediately transferred them to the thought capsule in the secret part of my mind; my tiny container of intelligence, like a private microchip, kept well away from the danger of influencing my official thoughts.

I had perfected the look of earnest approval with no display of facial expression. I had learned to emanate. Some of the others were overdoing it, occasionally nodding vigorously, giving a little twitch of a fist, wrinkling the eyes into suppressed passion. All wrong. The face and the body must be inert, conveying nothing. Perhaps just a trace of alertness.

More than all the other people under constant scrutiny, I must do it perfectly.

The lecture was part of a new strategy. Instead of saying the same things in different ways, once a week we were given exactly the same lecture.

"There used to be lots of big and little countries, lots of religions, all arguing and fighting one another, keeping humanity weak. All gone now. Peace everywhere now. Now, they are all gone. Only the State remains. Only the State matters. All people are equal within their social groups. All are only members of the State. Everything is the State. Do not be deceived into thinking there is anything . . . out there, anywhere. All the things in the sky that you see at night are so many stones, of no use to anyone, like stones you might see as you walk along, to be ignored or cast aside. And there is no country, no political or religious movement, anywhere in the world to make a rebellion. No more rebellions, no more opposition to hold us all back. Only the State now, always advancing, always progressing. Eastern State, Western State, Central State. All part of the State. All people part of the State. Not *in* the State: *of* the State. All one thing.

"No magical beings telling you what to do and what not to do. Now there is something real to worship, to tell you what to do. The State is your God, your mother and your father, your protector, your teacher, your lover, your wise guide. It is you. The State is the stable rock, the most tangible of things; but also your great abstract, encircling you, and within you, ever present, ever knowing, incapable of being deceived by anyone. It sees and hears everything you do. For some of you, it sees and hears what you see and hear. And for a special few, it sees and hears what you think."

He smiled and shook his head, implying inexpressible admiration. "What an honour, what a privilege, for those special people who have been selected to participate in this great advancement."

I knew one person who hadn't been granted an honour or a privilege in having the ultimate guardian implanted. But I kept the thought in its capsule. Thoughts could rise to the surface and could be detected by those who were trained to look for the slightest signs of disapproval. In dismissing, aborting, the thought, I indulged in some quick glances at the whole audience, all with their backs to me. I was looking for the slightest signs of badthought. It could even be indicated by body posture. It was not acceptable for anyone to change a sitting position for blood flow or because of discomfort. Rigid immobility was confirmation both of absolute loyalty, absolute clarity of thought, absolute mastery over one's body and mind. That was why on the way to the assembly hall, I had delicately manoeuvred to the back of the crowd. I wanted to stand at the back, releasing me from the horrors of numbness and itching.

But even here, standing at the back with some other observers, I had to be careful about delicately shifting my weight from one leg to the other. I had already seen some sideways glances. All the students observed themselves. Children were raised to watch one another for any sign of nonconformity. For the very young, aberrations were called Little Treasons. Spotting a little treason was reported in the same way as reporting a lost thing or a piece of litter.

Citizen Teacher! Nesta Hosier complained about the weather.

Citizen Teacher! Magda Civitz was standing still, and might have been thinking.

Citizen Teacher! My father said 'Damn their rules'.

And there it was. Someone was busily observing me. After a couple of his glances, I calmly retaliated by tilting my head about the width of a hair, and glancing not at the boy's face, but at his shoes. Something specific. He looked away, beaten by my mind punch. I kept my glance for a substantiating second, then looked at the lecturer again.

It was one vast, grim game, in which everyone played, all the way from infancy to death. A constant mental manoeuvring and self-control; a perpetual self-checking system before every spoken word, every look, every step. Is that the right thing to say or do? Might it be misinterpreted? Does the act of checking imply a defect in me? In a hundredth of a second, these and other checks passed through the brain like electronic impulses. The brain operated with computer speed. And it was done so often, every moment of every day, that first it became an unconscious act; and second, it was applied even before thinking. Alone in bed, you checked your silent thoughts, censoring them, rejecting them, even before they could form into existence.

That was the vital step: not thought correction, but thought prevention. The thoughts never existed. Statecorrect had replaced religioncorrect. Through fear and indoctrination, people controlled themselves. Over and over, lecturers quoted the new Citizen President's claim that one day, State control would not be necessary, because people would become their own guardians.

As the Professor put it, "When you do your brainwashing successfully, people will wash their own brains."

That was true. But the State control would always be there, to make sure.

I had stepped, been lifted, out of that system, and then, over two and a half years, I had been taught to go back into it, but under my control. The Professor had created me, in the official records, and in my role. I was Javid Yong. With so little discussion amongst departments, divisions, regions, everything controlled by statistics and reports, my credentials would not be checked. Only the statistics, the records, mattered. They would never lie. Everywhere that anyone looked in the records, all the records, I existed, in the present and in the past. I had parents and grandparents, all dead, I had schools and qualifications, I had training courses. I had had a brief friendship with a girl who existed in the records. We had agreed to terminate our friendship on the grounds that we wanted to avoid any possible distraction from our commitment to the State. Shortly after that, she had died. It was necessary, she had served her purpose and must now be destroyed. The Professor smiled grimly as he murdered people who had never existed.

"But for the rest of you," the lecturer droned, "there is the daily challenge of self-assessing, of ensuring that you meet the State's requirements in every way. Eventually, you will reach, attain, the stage at which no checking will be required, because you will be fully-formed, no longer an individual, but a simple, tiny part of the State, thinking and doing only as the State requires you to think and do. Then, you will have attained almost perfection. It will be impossible for you to commit a crime, to do any wrong thing, because, in effect, you will not exist. You will have been dissolved into the State."

He made it sound so desirable. The young people absorbed it. There was some body movement now, but of excitement, of a tremendous yearning to attain almost perfection, and then to strive for perfection. This squirming was permitted and approved. But for only a few seconds. A slow nod of acknowledgement from the lecturer, and then immobility must be resumed. Any further movement would be instantly observed and entered in the record. Climbing back to respectability was an almost impossible task. As a slogan put it:

The stain of failure can never be completely removed.

Wash, scrub and dye; the stain would always be there, detectable under the microscope of scrutiny.

Anyone sent to a House of Correction would strive to return to forgiveness and acceptance. It did not work like that. There could be no redeeming, no forgiving. You could atone, and go on atoning, until the stain was concealed from normal microscopic vision. Perhaps, after years of exceptional efficiency, much denouncing, there might be a way to reinstatement. And that became your purpose in life: that far away speck of possibility. But the stain would always be there.

"Excellent lecture," said a voice beside me.

I turned, not hurriedly, looked at the person who had spoken, and paused for a fraction of a second. "Yes. Always so. I find his lecturers satisfying."

"It would be impossible to be otherwise."

A very slight tilt of the head. "There is no otherwise." A hint of reproof. My point was complete idiocy. I understood what she meant. But you always looked for slight openings into which to thrust your sharp words. Another slogan: *Everyone is your brother or your sister. And your enemy.*

"Of course," she said, slightly overdoing it. A silent nod would have been better. She might be worth watching, but I didn't know who she was. Open curiosity about a fellow student was bad. As the lecturer had said, she was no more than a part of the State; asking about her identity would be very much in opposition to this, implying that she had an existence outside the State. It would be a crime of implication by me, and a crime of collaboration by her if she provided the information.

I turned away, looking for the target. One back of the head amongst seventy-four backs of heads. Where the bullet traditionally went. But the State cared nothing for tradition. It didn't matter. Your eventual death was almost an irrelevance. Your mind would have died long before.

CHAPTER THREE

CREATING a record for me was a long and difficult task for the Professor, but integrating that record into my present location was very much more difficult, especially with so much depending on its being done exactly right. When the record existed fully, every piece in place, then it would never be challenged, because it was the record. But before that, the system's self-checking programmes had to be overcome. Every detail in my background story had to be meticulously entered into all the other information, without raising any anomalous twitches, setting off alarms. In this part of the process, everything was checked and verified by the State systems, in a constant state of electronic paranoia, suspecting everything, asking questions about everything. Forcing the information to verify itself. Not only could the State not tolerate errors, it could not tolerate the possibility of errors. I suppose that my earlier adventure had made them much more sensitive on the matters of infiltration, circumvention, and escape.

Javid Yong was an orphan. I had a couple of days at the Orphanage, and then my parents were assigned to me. Being a parent had become a very respectable job, with a lot of responsibility because parents were also very close observers. There was no way round that one, and all my work, observing and trying to recruit, would have to be done under the minute and constant scrutiny of the OGs, discs, cameras and microphones, all the other security officers, and my parents. And, of course, every other child and adult.

Two OGs stood outside my apartment block. I showed not the slightest interest in them as they passed the verification beam over me. To me, thoroughly trained, they were merely a small part of the system, not even important enough to be a nuisance.

"Okay," said one of the OGs, trying very hard to be important. The other one swung an arm, and the door of my block opened. I felt like a prisoner returning to his cell.

Going up the concrete steps, I met the man who lived across the landing. Not looking directly at me, he hurried past, as though afraid of contamination. It was nothing alarming: that was the standard procedure. No-one used any of the old greetings which were polite enquiries about one's health and circumstances. No one said Hello or Good morning. Very simply, having such an interest was not permitted. Only the State mattered. And you were merely parts of the State.

Everything came back to that. Your importance was your lack of importance; your existence was your non-existence.

The apartment was little more than several small rooms with hollow partitions. It was in one of the twenty blocks which had been quickly built by the State for the purpose of establishing accommodation for Citizen 3s with assigned parents. The blocks had been built so that every block looked at another block. The outer walls of the outer blocks had no windows. It was important that the residents all looked inwards, actually and symbolically, and saw only repetitions of their own apartments, of themselves. When you looked out of your window, you saw a blank window, or you saw another you, looking back at you.

"Citizen Mother," I said in my best mechanical voice.

"Citizen Son," said my mother. "How was the lecture?"

"It was satisfyingly informative."

Such exchanges always brought the same problems. Enthusiasm implied emotional instability; saying that one had benefited implied earlier defects. There was a constant search for ways of expressing approval of everything that the State provided, while speaking of everything as though it were the dullest mediocrity, which it always was.

"Baked beans and rice tonight. Wash."

No-one could ever say there was a struggle to provide nourishing meals. Research and choice were not required. The menu was decided by the State, and the meals for each week were made available at the start of each week. It all came from tins and packets, and the lack of variety meant that we were rarely short of anything.

Baked beans and rice. Oh, well. It was food. Mustn't grumble. How many generations had that joke passed down? And now had been changed. An old stoical way of thinking had now become a State rule. Not written down anywhere, but everyone knew what would happen if you were heard grumbling.

My Mother had found that out the hard way.

After the baked beans and rice, it was rice pudding. With no sugar or milk, it wasn't a pleasant end to the meal. But I reminded myself that I wasn't here to be a miserable boy trapped in this terrible new world: I was a spy and recruiting agent, trained, physically and mentally, to do specific and important work.

It was ironical that so many millions, even billions, were being indoctrinated and forced to act unquestioningly to do whatever their leaders wanted them to do, having been indoctrinated to believe that their leaders were always right; and *I* was willing to do anything for *my* leader, never doubting that *he* was right. But *they* were all wrong, and *I* was right. He *was* right.

They believed the same, in reverse. So how could I know that they were wrong, and I was right? First, because of what had happened to me. My parents had been taken away, my best friend and I had been tortured, and she had been operated on to remove the last shred of privacy and individuality. Second, because of what I had been taught by the Professor: real history, real science, real everything. And truth about the State, the people who controlled the life of every human being.

"It is gymnastics tonight. Do I have your permission to attend?"

"Yes." As it was part of the compulsory training programme, parents couldn't refuse; but as a grotesque form of politeness, one always asked.

With his astonishing foresight, the Professor had put an obscure muscle problem on my record, and one acted session had been sufficient to convince the trainers that I was not suited to gymnastics. Therefore, I was required to watch and enjoy those who were sufficiently supple and intimidated to participate. Being in character, as I must always be, I could try to spot some defects in my neighbours and fellow pupils. Reporting a few people would help in the maintaining of my disguise. Perhaps the target would be there, and I could look for defects which I hoped weren't there, but which were clues to his suitability for recruitment. I was looking for subtleties within the subtleties, secrets which even the secrets couldn't see.

The school wasn't far away. Nothing was far away. Everything was subject to a controlled insularity, and precisely centralised in each district. People were better controlled when they didn't go travelling. And when they did travel, they needed to have an excellent, authorised, reason ready when challenged. Even the shortest journey would be done by the shortest possible route. If you tried to justify a detour by saying that you wanted to look at the river, or a particular tree, or the sunset, it would always lead to the question: 'Why?' That was more effective than an accusation or a complaint, or even a threat; because the question required an explanation, and it was almost impossible to do this without incriminating yourself, even after a succession of questions leading from the first one. The only way out of it was to have an explanation ready, one which had nothing to do with the real reason. The simplest one was to say that you saw someone who looked suspicious, and followed him, or her. If they pressed for details, it was better to shake your head and say that you were mistaken. It might all sound suspicious, but there was nothing that you had actually done wrong.

On this occasion, I didn't do an actual detour. I stopped under a small tree which had surprisingly escaped the great cull of trees and bushes during the State campaign to keep the countryside out of the city. No distractions, no blurring of categories. That's there, this is here, and that's how they'll stay. Besides, countryside in the city might encourage people to feel slightly more benevolent, even relaxed; and that would never do.

"Report," Katina said, as she always did. She was fully in the role, too, determined not to give me the slightest encouragement to go out of character.

"Training lecture attended. Target observed. No weakness noticed. Surveillance continuing as planned. I'm having to be patient."

"That is what we want and expect."

"Now school gymnastics. An opportunity for general observation."

"I'll report."

I couldn't see her, and didn't look up. She was hovering in the branches, and had her own ways of coming and going. I was not to enquire or try to see her. We were to stay in character, always. I think this coldness was the most difficult part of my deception. She was my weakness, as it were. I was too fond of her, too dependent on her in every crisis. And she was my link to our secret place with the Professor, high in the mountain. She made me feel homesick. For that reason, I was glad when she didn't reply to my acknowledgement of her last comment. She was gone, and I could resume being a nasty, egotistic Citizen 3.

We were all 'citizens' now, even the youngest children. A vital part of the early implanting of the belief that the individual didn't count. All the way up to the Citizen President.

Citizen Teacher Kemp was waiting at the door. He almost stood to attention as he snapped, "Citizen Student!" Never 'Good evening": all evenings were good under the State.

"Citizen Teacher!" I snapped it back at him.

"Row 4, Seat 35!"

So dramatic. How to respond? Never thank anyone for doing his or her job. If in doubt, go for obedience and neutrality combined. I did a little bow.

Now came a new feature. A disgraced Citizen 2, still in green to show what he had been, but with a brown bib to show what he was now, hurried forward to show me to my seat. It wasn't necessary, but this burden of pointless tasks was part of the punishment by humiliation. Any show of resentment, even of defiant dignity, was strictly forbidden. Abject servility must be shown at all times.

"This way, Citizen Student. A very good seat. Excellent view."

I wanted to slap his face and tell him to stop it. Instead, I said nothing as he led me to my seat and shuffled away. I sat and looked round, still with the look of contempt. It was disappointing that people were so firmly fastened into their subservience and fear that it was difficult to detect any defects. People had become smoothly functioning robots, without thought or feeling.

Reaching that condition could be done easily, with the right incentives.

It was happening to me.

It was the only way.

As people went to their seats, there were no comments, no smiles, no apologies for treading on someone's foot, no complaints about being trodden on. Just empty functioning.

And yet, in the appropriate circumstances, each of these empty vessels could change in a moment into a vicious bully, a vindictive plotter, a raging proclaimer of the power and purity of the State. What you did, what you *were*, was strictly controlled by the State.

If the State told you to laugh, you laughed.

If the State told you to cry, you cried.

And if the State told you to be empty, but scrutinise everyone around you, that was what you did. All the time, you watched, you detected weaknesses, you reported.

Someone looked at me. Not the usual constant scrutiny, for which one was always prepared, always blankly suggesting nothing but loyal obedience. This was something else. This had a brief, laser-like intensity, so strong that I continued to feel it after the observer had turned away.

I was so shocked that I continued to stare.

Two years after I had last seen it, I still knew that face so well.

Elika Plenty.

Or what remained of her after they had altered her.

CHAPTER FOUR

"No! Not at all, not in any way. She is not yet in the plan."

It was the response that I'd expected, but when I decided to test the water, I didn't expect to be drowned. But Katina was in her stern mood.

"You must stay focused all the time. There must be no deviations, no digressions, no wandering off from the path of the plot."

Very clearly expressed. Actually, the last bit was almost poetic.

She hadn't finished. "Even asking questions, making suggestions is dangerous. You must not try to step in and out of your role. It won't work. It's all or nothing. No compromises, no compassion, no curiosity. Now, do your job as instructed and agreed."

"Sorry."

"Don't apologise," she almost shrieked.

"Sor . . . yes. You're right. Very brief lapse. Part of the process, not to be repeated. Now, go back and report."

As I walked away from the shadow of a wall, I mentally pushed Elika into the void. She was an irrelevance. So were my parents. I must be cold and ruthless. I was on my way to school.

That was all. I must be without compassion. I must be without distracting thoughts.

Different subjects, different teachers, had different deliveries. Citizen Teacher Shaw's were the slow flow of stagnant history, the repetition of what we all knew; whereas Citizen Teacher Harbin's State Economics lessons of statistical information were like hailstones on a tin roof. His information was certain to be as false as Mrs Shaw's, but the numbers clattered into the brain, taking on even more the appearance of truth. And the numbers all proved that the State was doing wonderfully well, because of the leadership which we were privileged to have over us. A neutral observer might have wondered why, in view of the State's constant superlative performance, it was always improving on the previous performances. The Professor knew that every month, every quarter, every year, the previous period's figures were reduced, ensuring constant statistical improvement.

Simultaneously, Mr Harbin recited grim warnings about the State's poverty. Basically, the State had plenty of money for extravagant projects, but no money for the simple necessities. It could build motorways, but it couldn't provide enough food. Except rice, beans and sardines.

Mr Harbin didn't explain or analyse, not the successes or the failures; he merely recited the achievements and problems, as indications of financial reality, even though the indications were contradictions. Well, accepting contradictions was an essential part of the control of people.

After the lesson, I manoeuvred myself close to Mikel, and coughed. Not a hinting cough, just an ordinary cough to clear the throat. He half turned and glanced in my direction. I couldn't be sure that he had looked at me, or even seen me, other than as another student in the crowd.

"You did not daydream, Citizen Student Yong."

Breakthrough.

I turned to Mikel and said, "No, Citizen Student Brovnik. I

concentrated on receiving the valuable and interesting information."

"That was wise. Don't let thoughts intrude."

Another glance, with a slightly increased intensity. That comment about thoughts could have been a simple State maxim, but it could also have been a deliberately ironical statement,

The next step was to work out what the next step should be.

I didn't have to work it out. As we walked along, I saw Elika walking in the opposite direction. She was in a group of students, clearly heading for her next lesson. She looked towards me, but gave no sign of recognition. I gave her only a quick glance, but perhaps there was some intensity in the glance because Mikel said, "Most Model Student for last two months. Inspiration to us all."

"Oh? Which one is she?" I asked clumsily.

"Don't you know Citizen Student Plenty?"

"Oh, yes. I do recognise her now. I've seen award photographs."

"And her famous presentation in The Red Hall last month."

"Ah, yes."

"It's all but settled that she will be Sister Virtue in our production of The Triumph of the State. I'm hoping for a part. What about you?"

"I . . . I'm not any good at acting."

"Really? I'd have thought you were very good at it. Ah. Ready for some *Recognition of our Enemies*?"

"Yes." The word crept out through my furry throat.

"Very important lesson. Spies, infiltrators, saboteurs everywhere, in disguises. Good actors, no doubt. I am determined to find any that are around here."

As we entered the classroom, I became aware that I was soaked with sweat.

CHAPTER FIVE

"THEY ARE ALL AROUND YOU. Spies are everywhere."

The teacher was almost quoting Mikel word for word. But it wasn't surprising with such a simple, inflexible warning. Most teaching was by repetition and reinforcement. I remembered my father once, long ago, hammering a nail into a door frame, and continuing to hammer after the nail was firmly embedded, below the surface of the wood; still he hammered, as though he needed to hammer away all doubts that the nail would stay in place.

"Trust no-one!" The teacher looked at me, and for a terrible moment I expected the class to turn and look at me. Was my face showing the heat of guilt? I took the standard evasion by looking about me suspiciously. When I looked over a back, I raised my head slightly, as though moving in for a closer scrutiny.

For how many centuries had this method been used? Declare your innocence by directing attention to the possible guilt of others. Innocence was virtually impossible to prove, and guilt could be proved in an instant. A wrong word, a wrong look, a wrong body gesture. But how did you prove innocence? Not being accused of doing wrong wasn't enough; constantly doing the right things wasn't enough. That merely put you on the same level as everyone else, and could be covering your guilt. And a previously innocent person, even over many years, could destroy all that innocence by one misdemeanour. Instantly guilty, but a lifetime of remorse and repentance could never quite remove the stain.

At higher levels, treachery became huge and awful; at our level, it was just a perverted conception of being naughty, and punishment was merely citizenship training, making us better people, part of the indoctrination of never deviating by a hair's breadth from the way of the State.

I left the classroom with a deliberately slow pensiveness, suggesting that I was not eager to leave.

"Citizen Student Yong!"

I looked up and round, startled. "Citizen Teacher!" I strode quickly to the teacher's desk.

"You look thoughtful. Thinking is bad. Only learning truth of State is good. What were you thinking about?"

"Citizen Teacher, I was thinking of ways to trap spies and traitors. I regret this, and will not do it again."

For a flicker of a moment, I could see a collision of thoughts inside his head, a contradiction of policies, of ideas, of rules, which was not allowed. Thinking was wrong, but was thinking right things wrong? He untangled the dilemma and said, "What you thought about was not wrong, but the act of thinking is dangerous. It can lead to bad thoughts. Therefore, all thinking is necessarily bad because of its potential to lead to bad thoughts."

"Citizen Teacher, the clarity of your generous explanation removes all trace of that failure in me. It will not happen again."

A slight nod. "Go to your next lesson, Citizen Student Yong."

I bowed and walked away in a manner which, I hoped, suggested no thought, not even about the clear explanation.

And outside, there was Mikel, standing still, watching me. "Citizen Student Yong. Did you receive additional guidance?"

"Yes, Citizen Student Brovnik. It was needed and provided. I am a better citizen for it."

How could I talk in this ridiculous way? It was easy from the moment that it became a necessary habit. When reality and thought are forbidden, and only the propaganda and certain permitted ways of speaking are permitted, choices and confusions disappear. Provided that all thoughts and instincts are suppressed, or cease to exist, life becomes very easy. The State had assumed the status of a godless religion, in which all temptations had been removed.

In that moment, in which the dark shadow of despair seemed to obliterate the plan, we held each other's direct look. Just for that moment. People no longer looked into, or even at, one another's eyes. To do so suggested personalities. You looked at the representation of a person in a uniform. You looked at a forehead, a collar, a space just beyond the head, never into eyes.

And that was precisely what we had done. Not a brief look: it was a signal. Knowing, instinctively, that tiptoeing must occasionally be followed by a big step forward, I risked the slightest of nods. He responded in the same way.

Contact!

I walked away decisively, another small gesture to show that I was doing what was necessary. I ignored him, never looking out of the narrow perspective of straight ahead, all the way to the next lesson. This was a short and easy one to finish the day, all about food health, the whole lesson showing with short films and statistics how the food which the State provided was the most nutritious. Beans and rice was the best meal for proteins and starches. Sardines provided vitamins and minerals, now that the sea had been cleared of the capitalists' pollution. It was really a menu justification, and more self-adulation by the State.

I made myself look keen, but never surprised, all through the lesson, then thanked the teacher and bowed. We all left without a show of enthusiasm. It was impolite, and an offence, to show a keenness to be out and away. In my case, there was no cause for enthusiasm. Life with my appointed parents was dull and irritating. But I wasn't aware of how slowly I was walking, left well behind, until a familiar voice said, "You are thinking, Citizen Student Yong."

It was a frightening moment. Staying in control, I said, "I was merely reviewing the excellent lesson. Not thinking."

"Ah. That is good. Thinking is dangerous. Don't you think?"

In spite of all the danger, his clever playing with words, and what it implied, made me release a little tension with a smile.

He raised an eyebrow. "Be careful, Citizen Student Yong. Smiling at each other would be the sort of thing to bring an OG, seething with official indignation."

"You are right. And articulate. I advise that we separate. Talking, loitering, are also offences."

"Before we part. I have watched you as you have watched me. I trust you. Do you trust me?"

"I do."

"Goodbye, Citizen Student Yong."

"Goodbye, Citizen Student Brovnik."

Katina was pleased, but still cautious.

"It isn't just a matter of whether or not he can be trusted: it's whether or not they are already watching him, and listening to him."

"If they were, wouldn't it be too late now?"

There was a pause. "The Professor acknowledges your point. But he wants you to be aware that they would go for you first, keeping Mikel as the lure until the last moment. Therefore, there might be no indication of detection until they pounce."

That wasn't a pleasant thought. Deceiving me, or deceiving them, Mikel was a double danger. Or a danger with two parts. It wasn't just a case of how I could know, but of how *he* could know. Since having my IG fitted when I was twelve, I had received several mandatory vaccinations. But how did I know what was put in me? I didn't look at the needle being put in, so they could have inserted a disease, a micro-receiver, or even a micro-camera. The State told you to report for vaccination, and that's what you did. Generally, I was a light, restless sleeper, but very occasionally I was surprised to have a deep sleep. How did I know why I had a deep sleep? How did I know whether something was done to me while I slept.

Someone could be listening to everything that Mikel and I said to each other, as the State played a deadly game with us, enticing us on, letting the incriminating evidence grow steadily, waiting for the moment when it was time to end the game, and drag us in, and start the interrogations. And this time, they would be simple tortures, with no pretence of trying to make me a better person. They wouldn't want remorse, repentance, recanting. They would want only information. Not information just to help them: this would be information to destroy the final opposition. It would be the end of all thought, except the rigid strategy thought of the elite, as they endlessly devised ways of stopping and preventing all thought.

How long would it take before I shouted that it was the Professor who had arranged it all, and told them the location of his domain?

I said, "Katina, we have talked about caution, we have planned caution, and we have used great caution. But now, as I am about to take this big step, I need to know, for my sake and yours, is there a plan for my rescue?"

There was another pause as she listened to the Professor. "A rescue of the sort that we arranged before would keep you from torture, or the worst of it, and it would keep the location and what we have still secret; but it would alert them to the danger of infiltration, and they would be much more careful about the appearance of new people, probably less trusting of their computer records. It would be much better, for all of us, if we could arrange for your removal in the most subtle manner, without its being clearly a rescue. You would disappear. After a few days, the records would show that you had presumably drowned in a river, the suggestion being suicide."

"In either case, it would be nice to have an alarm thing on which I could call you."

She metaphorically shook her head. "There are too many electronic devices through which you must go, at school, in the streets, in the lecture hall. Most of the time, you aren't aware of them, but they are there, sending their little beams at you. Just as I'd be detected, so would an alarm device. To the security beams, it would be the equivalent of a foreign body in your blood, alerting your antibodies."

"I know. I hadn't forgotten. I was just being wistful, rueful."

"And hoping the Professor would change his mind."

"Yes."

"No more of that. You have been thoroughly trained by the Professor to behave as someone who has been thoroughly trained by the State. Stay in character, even when talking with me."

"Yes, Citizen Teacher."

"Excellent. Go, quickly. OGs in the area."

There certainly were. Two walking together, another across the way. I stared straight ahead, not looking guilty, not looking like someone who was trying not to look guilty, not looking aloof, just focused on the State, and my next task for the State. A good little robot.

Except that *good* and *bad* no longer existed as moral standards, only in their meaning of loyal to the State, and treacherous to the State. And everyone was clear about what each one meant.

CHAPTER SIX

Citizen Principal looked at me, frowning, as he said, "You have been reported by teachers, pupils and even Outer Guardians as being solitary, aloof, walking on your own. This is not good."

It was difficult to respond to this complaint, but I should have been prepared. *Everyone is your enemy.* It was an important part of State control to force everyone into groups, self-monitoring clusters, in which even subversive thoughts could be detected. And trying to avoid that was even more subversive. *Bad thoughts find the one who walks alone.*

This situation called for some good old Lanny waffle. "It is true, Citizen Principal. Thinking is bad, but I can't help thinking of ways in which I can be a better student of the State."

"Not walking alone and thinking would be one good way."

Well, quite. "Yes, sir. In trying to be better, I have been worse. I resolve to improve, and ask for special training in this."

That was a smart move, asking the education man for some training. He would have a course for every defect. It would be combined with punishment, as most education was, but it counted as education, and therefore counted as one of his specialities. And he was being involved in the special education process. A supplier, as it were.

He wrinkled the brow and pursed the lips as he pondered. I made myself refrain from pondering. Going on a training and punishment course was certainly not what I wanted, for obvious reasons, but this is the big problem with desperate improvising. The vital thing was to keep my pretence intact and the big plan secret. To do that, staying in character, I had no choice but to be a repentant student. Arguing, defending myself, pretending that I wasn't aware, of the rule or of breaking the rule; all these were not permissible, and would anger, which in turn would attract the most suspicious surveillance.

On the other hand, going on an education course might lead to surveillance. I had done the opposite of what I had been instructed to do: I had drawn attention to myself. No doubt, there would be a reprimand from Katina, when I had taken the risk of isolating myself in order to speak with her.

"Yes. I think this course will suit you well. Achievement through Collective Harmony."

I forced a blank look of pleasure onto my face. It hung there, trying not to slide off. "Yes, Citizen Principal. That is what I need."

"It will be arranged."

I managed to keep my body erect as I left, but it felt limp. I went to one of the Katina trees, and waited. Not for long. She was always hovering nearby, ready to join me. I explained.

There was no reprimand. "This is what was inevitable. If you performed perfectly, you wouldn't make any progress with Mikel. But you must behave impeccably on the course. No protests, no resentment. Accept pain and the many discomforts as being necessary."

Very glib, but sort of reassuring.

She hadn't quite finished. "Endure, and do your best acting."

"Katina," I said. "You inspire me to great things."

"That is good," she replied.

I quickly walked away.

"Why are you all on this training course?"

Citizen Teacher Lye had a very sharp and penetrating voice, and she was another of the angry ones that I knew so well.

The response was silence. Well, if you make people afraid of speaking, and virtually forbid thinking, what do you expect?

"Well?"

I called, "Citizen Teacher. To become as we should be."

She wanted to find fault with that, and shout something disparaging; but in its vagueness, it was right. But no-one was allowed to have a successful moment. We had to be wrong, even about being right.

"To be MADE as you should be. There is no becoming. You are mis-shapes. You will be pushed, squeezed, pulled, and beaten if necessary, into the right shape. All of you into one shape. Like a key which must be exactly right to open a door."

Nicely put. I stared with what I hoped was a submissive, but determined, look of conformity. Doing these simultaneous, often contradicting, responses was exhausting. Life must be so much simpler when you stopped all resistance, emptied your brain of everything but what the State put there, and just let everything happen as the State demanded. No acting, no pretending, no deceit, no covering of tracks. The State poured its lies into you, and you poured them out again. There was a constant supply, in and out, in and out. Artificial facts and slogans, consumed and regurgitated.

"Right. Twenty-four of you. Form into four groups of six, in four lines."

On the simple basis of practicality, I didn't join the shufflers. Citizen Teacher Lye glared. "Citizen Student Yong! Why aren't you joining a group as instructed?"

"Citizen Teacher, I am in a group."

"Oh? Which one?"

"The one which has five members."

Of course this was wrong, strategically. I was supposed to be someone whose brain had been permanently numbed long ago. Using my intelligence, and explaining it, were bad things, punishable things. It was my own personality thrusting through my disguise. With a shock, I realised that *I* was the biggest danger to me. This egotistical personality, always being a smarty, always trying to outdo people. At this rate, the Professor's great plan would soon be destroyed, and I'd either be killed or severely altered, as Elika had been.

"You are insolent!"

I bowed. "I am filled with remorse, Citizen Teacher. I was trying to be economical with resources, and exercise strict control. I failed."

"*I* control! Not you! You are just a puny, worthless failure student. That is why you are here. To be forced into your proper shape. Not to have (she wriggled her fingers) puny thoughts. Go to your group."

I bowed again, turned and went to the back of the one-short queue. But I told myself sternly that there must be no more aberrations. That *must* be the last one.

The problem, as we played team game after team game, was in being a convincing, numbed-brain robot, while being an enthusiastic participant in group activities. Should I try to lead, or merely follow? After a little while, I rescued myself from this dilemma by the simple means of recalling why I had been put here by Citizen Principal. I was supposed to be changing into a fully sociable person, always wanting to be in a group. These were team games. Right, then.

"Let's go round the group, and take a turn to say what we think. How does that sound?"

Oh, resentment. Lots of glares and frowns. Never mind that. "If we all work together, we'll solve the problem together. Citizen Student Harris. What do you think?"

"I think we should ask ourselves what our Leadership would do."

"Good. Citizen Student Middy?"

"I think we should consult The Way to Good Citizenship."

So it went on. When the other five had said what they thought, with furtive glances towards the supervising teacher, I said, "I think we should attach the four pieces to one another, and then fasten the rope to the pole. Shall we try that?"

They looked at the pieces lying on the grass as though they had just arrived from space. The actual point of the exercise lay there, and all they could suggest was variations on doing it in a way that the State would approve. And that wasn't working as a team. I ignored the teacher, and began to assemble the poles. The whole thing was so easy. It required the minimum of thought.

But was that too much thought? Had I blundered again?

I attached the rope, and at last looked towards the teacher. "Citizen Teacher. A team effort," I said.

She raised an eyebrow. Of course it wasn't. "Go on to the next challenge," she said.

Having briefly been the leader, I was now shoved aside, as the group imitated my democratic method, but changed it to having a self-assertive leader in Citizen Student Harris, and the rest with specific functions. A fully organised team. By the end of the challenge, the pieces still lay on the grass. I had been appointed 'post-challenge reviewer', which meant that I wasn't to participate. The rest had all been allocated formal roles which might have sounded impressive, but bore no connection to the task. Citizen Harris had appointed the equivalent of department heads, but no-one to work on the problem. I decided to leave them to it this time, adopting a passive role to display my membership of the team.

The problem wasn't solved. Any one of them could have done it if their brains hadn't been put into sleep mode. They had been taught the importance of organising and appointing, not of doing. If they had been left long enough, they would have arranged meetings to discuss different methods of approaching the problem of the pieces on the grass. Not to discuss how to do it, but what method to use. Meetings to discuss how to do it would come much later.

But why? Why all this inactive, ineffective behaviour? Because even if anything remotely rebellious occurred to a large number of people, they would be incapable of doing anything without meetings and consultations. Direct, innovative, impetuous behaviour had been trained out of them. I doubted that any of the leaders wanted us to solve the problems, or cared whether or not we did. What they wanted was what had just happened: the group settling into a socially agreeable torpor, in which nothing was achieved. As the Professor had said, *What isn't achieved is just as important as what is achieved, so long as it's done in the approved way.*

In that case, I took a deep breath, and stood erect, ready to do nothing with enthusiastic vigour. Here I come, my leaders, a willing idiot. Watch me participate in the team, contributing nothing but my eager participation.

For the rest of my time, that is what I did. I warmed to the task. I was everywhere that there were people congregating. I babbled about State developments, the pleasure of eating rice, the thrill of being here, performing all these activities together. I was a thoroughly annoying bore.

An occasional subtle glance showed that the teachers approved.

And I wasn't punished once.

CHAPTER SEVEN

WORK TRAINING WAS NOW a regular formal part of the curriculum. For two days a week, I worked in a factory. Silver linings and all that, it was much better than a mill, where I had worked before. It was tedious, mundane and brain-numbingly repetitive, but it was safe. There was even a small canteen which provided snacks during a half hour rest period.

It wasn't so much a factory as the loading bay at the end of the factory process. Containers emerged from a rectangular pit, packaged items were put in the containers, and they were then moved on trolleys by the student workers to be sealed, then put in the vehicles which would distribute them. It was a vast building, but empty of everything except people, containers and the various vehicles and bits of equipment.

There were supervisors, foremen and forewomen, who checked that everything was being done correctly; which, in view of the simplicity of the task, was usually the case. This meant that there wasn't the usual compulsion to shout and complain. But managers were another matter. Everything was always wrong, because everything must always be wrong. That was their notion, the State's notion, of management. The containers were badly loaded onto the trolleys, badly unloaded from the trolleys, and badly loaded onto the vehicles. The work wasn't done quickly enough. It wasn't done smoothly enough. And eventually, the students became so nervous that mistakes were made.

And when the managers complained, the supervisors thought that they should complain; and in a few minutes, a well-organised operation descended into ill-tempered, neurotic chaos.

Through Katina, the Professor informed me that this was not entirely a State defect, being an old and basic management failing. If there was no nothing to manage, why have a manager? So managers created problems in order to be seen to be managing something. It was just that these new managers had a new line in aggression and the finding of faults.

The physical work was doubly beneficial: exercise, and release from the incessant indoctrination. There were times when I stopped thinking about anything, which was another pleasure.

After a day of manual labour, I went home feeling hungry, but there I was still the assigned student, and the menu was stipulated, and the budget trimmed, so the hungry man had to revert to the obedient boy, grateful for his meagre portion of beans and rice.

Then, it was up to the bedroom as usual, and back into thinking about what I needed to do. The necessary constant slow subtlety combined with the necessary urgency was very disrupting. The State had had infiltrators in their places operating for years, trickling their indoctrination into the ears of the gullible and misinformed. But they weren't in constant danger of exposure and punishment. Everything that they wanted to kill or ban was working in their favour while they planned and prepared. Freedom of speech, freedom of movement, democratic choices, compassion; all these combined to provide the soft fertile ground in which the enemy could grow without any hindrance.

"Today, we have a special lecture for you," said Citizen Teacher Sims, "a special presentation. By Citizen Model Student Plenty."

I made my mask one of mild interest. Surely that was acceptable for a presentation by a several times model student. I had to do *something* with my face. I couldn't trust the expressionless blank which I wore most of the time. I think what bothered me most was the prospect of seeing and hearing her in her altered state. I didn't know what else they did now, but more than two years ago, they had done everything to her. In addition to the constantly monitoring and reporting Inner Guardian, they had inserted a camera which showed them what she was seeing.

Had they done more? Had they penetrated, invaded, her brain, and taken up residence there?

Did they even need to?

Elika had been sitting behind the teacher, but now he moved aside and told her to come forward. At least I was justified in looking at her, the model student, because everyone else was. I even felt a small twinge of jealousy. They didn't deserve her. But then I remembered that it wasn't really Elika. They'd inserted their thing, and no doubt done other things to her, to make her a model student, about to do a presentation.

She said in a clear voice, "You see before you a two times model student, and you are impressed. So you should be. But I wasn't always a model student. I was a very long way from that. You could say that I was the opposite. I rebelled against our beautiful State. I thought I knew better. I thought that others knew better. Well, they were all leading me astray, trying to separate me from my original and true goal, to serve the State.

"I was punished, over and over, in Houses of Correction, but still I followed the wrong course. Until the time that I had the Final Step, my enlightenment. And at last. I saw the error of my ways, my foolishness in fighting a system which wanted only to give the best to me, by receiving the best *from* me. The two things are connected, both State and I, giving and receiving.

"And now my life is fulfilling, happy, and beautiful. And

yours can be, too. Sign up for the Final Step, to make model students of all of you. Yes, *all* of you."

So, now, it even had a name.

She smiled benignly at us, and her soft gaze moved slowly round the room. I told myself to look slightly away, to concentrate on the wall behind her, on Citizen Teacher Sims; anything, anywhere, but not directly at her when she looked at me.

And then I looked directly at her, meeting her gaze, looking into her eyes. Of all the many stupid things that I'd done so far in my whole life, this was by far the most stupid. Our eyes met. I tried to distract her by looking at her chin while drawing myself up, thrusting out my chest, trying to look like a typical student, eager to please.

Her gaze continued round.

Citizen Teacher Sims stepped forward. "Thank you for that, Citizen Student Plenty. Clear and concise, but inspiring. I have no doubt that every student in this room will volunteer for the special treatment."

The students were indulging in permitted restlessness, twitching and bouncing around in their eagerness to sign up, for what I presumed would be insertion of the micro-cameras in their brains. That was the detail which wasn't included in Elika's presentation, which contained almost no substance. She had been sent to recruit. How could she ever refuse? They knew where she went, what she heard, what she saw. How could she not comply, and then obey every command?

And, most terrible thought, perhaps she *wanted* to recruit, to persuade, to convince. Perhaps she now believed that it was the best thing to do.

How altered was she?

Did she have her memory? I wanted her to remember me, but it was essential that she didn't. At least not well enough to link me to the physically altered person who would shortly be so close to her.

Recruiting was done in the old-fashioned way, with every

student going to the front of the class and providing his or her name. This sort of thing could be done electronically, but doing it this way emphasised the act, and gave it a form of symbolism. Citizen Teacher Sims was taking our names, while Elika sat watching us, still smiling. Presumably, the prolonged benign smile of a successful recruiter was permitted. It was probably encouraged. Even in the days of my secret, private rebellion, an event such as this would have excited me. Especially with my favourite person exhorting us to join.

There was no question of not volunteering. Whenever the State was recruiting, volunteering was mandatory. Besides, I'd have been the only one to refuse. But I waited for my turn as though I were the most patient and polite person on Earth. Perhaps something would happen to prevent it.

It didn't. My turn came. "Citizen Student Javid Yong." Full name for something like this. I lowered my voice.

"Don't mumble!" Citizen Teacher Sims snapped. "Speak loudly and clearly."

"Citizen Student Javid Yong," I said with defiant force.

Elika looked up, but not at me, slightly to the side of me. As I returned to my seat, Citizen Teacher Sims called, "An excellent response from this class. I'm sure you all wish to express your gratitude to Citizen Student Plenty.

We all stood and in unison called, "Thank you, Citizen Student Plenty." Elika gave a solemn little bow. Citizen Teacher Sims looked pleased. There was no smile, just the modest satisfaction of having done his job well.

There was a brief postscript announcement, which I was pleased to hear. "Because the operation is a complex and difficult one, requiring a lot of technical considerations, the operation will be done one at a time, with a couple of days allowed for checking for any adverse reactions, so you will have to be patient in waiting for your turn."

The lesson now began. The subject was social responsibility. After Citizen Teacher Sims had provided a list of achievements by volunteers, each student had to stand and say what he or she was doing, intended to do, or had done, to assist in the great cause of the State. For the purpose of volunteer work, the State was in its poverty role. Citizen Student Mings, almost bursting with importance, informed us that every night this week, he had rushed home from school, had a quick tea, then rushed out to the smelting works in the next district, where they were happy to have his free services.

"That is commendable, Citizen Student Mings. What job do you do?"

"I do whatever is needed that I am able to do. Most of the time, I'm a bucket carrier, pouring water on the molten rods."

My little bit of imaginary civic duty was deliberately mediocre and vague in order to discourage checks. I claimed that I had been going round the streets, picking up litter, and putting it in the bins.

Not good enough. "But litter is forbidden now. It was the capitalists who threw litter all over the streets."

"Yes, Citizen Teacher. But things accidentally become litter when the wind picks them up, carries them and drops them in our streets."

"Ah. I see. No, that is not litter. That is windtake. Very different. You must have been told the difference. Windtake and watertake are not litter."

I must have missed that lesson. And many more. "Yes, Citizen Teacher. I think that in my eagerness to do a good thing, I forgot that."

He actually gave a small shrug. "Though you were inept, your intention was acceptable. Find another thing to report on in the next lesson."

I felt the indignation of someone who *had* been picking up litter. In my mind, I had been working very hard for days. How dare they declare it to be useless!

But at least I had been given a mild, almost sympathetic, response by Citizen Teacher Sims. That recruitment success had put him in a good mood. At least he had one. He didn't smile, but his bland features were devoid of the usual stern frown, giving him a round-faced innocence. When the lesson ended, and we had thanked him, we filed out. I gave the briefest of glances towards Elika. She sat with her back rigidly straight, her eyes looking well away from me. Just as well, I thought, remembering that what *she* saw, *they* saw.

What a depressing thought that was. Katina and the Professor were right to tell me to keep away. There would come a time, but this wasn't it, and it was a long way off yet.

And I had no idea how it could be done.

CHAPTER EIGHT

JUST FOR A CHANGE, Katina next appeared, or didn't appear, in a bush. I was on my way to the first of my two days of work each week at a factory. Looking on the bright side, it was very much better work than in my previous life as Lanny. I was doing different parts of the process of moving plastic and cardboard boxes, from one part of a large warehouse to another, and from there onto the great transporters. It was repetitive and tedious, and apart from occasional moments of idiocy, not dangerous. But it was very busy, and very crowded, with millions of cardboard and plastic boxes, and hundreds of, it seemed to me, cardboard and plastic people.

I pretended to tie my shoelaces, and checked that there were no discs nearby.

Apart from sharing my curiosity about what they might have done to Elika, Katina was not interested in her. That was a peripheral matter. A possible distraction. She spoke with a touch of sternness. I almost suggested that she was jealous of Elika, but there are some things you don't say to your robot helper. It wouldn't be right.

As an example of the possible distraction element, she

pointed out that I was now in a rather worrying predicament. Having volunteered for the Final Step, there was a pretty strong chance that I'd soon find myself in a line of willing volunteers waiting to have the Final Step done to me.

"Yes, well, of course that's the major concern. I was just taking things in reverse priority order."

"So have you started to think about ways of extricating yourself?"

"I thought something like that should be discussed before any decisions are made."

"Yes. But an effective discussion should be formed around the members' suggestions. However, our suggestion is that you try to be inconspicuous for a few days while we think about this new problem."

"Katina. If it came down to a straight choice of losing me or the plan, which would you choose?"

"You must be constantly alert. It is essential that any retreat, escape, rescue, is not performed openly, as it was last time. You must leave well before that point arrives. You must leave silently, invisibly, in such a way that your departure does not look like a retreat, escape, rescue. The Professor could then create a suicide record for you. But even that would be difficult, because he would be creating a current record instead of a past one."

"Katina! I have been taking orders all the time that I have been here, and through all my training; but I think the time has come for you and the Professor to admit that this has been a colossal blunder. You, he, should have seen the probability of this occurring. Conformity and control in and over everything were bound to lead to this problem."

Another of those mini-pauses, then Katina said, "The Professor says that you are right. In his obsessive desire, even he allowed himself to look away from this obvious point in the plan. He will not abandon you, but he needs time to work this out. You must do whatever you can to stall." Another brief pause, which in this circumstance seemed ominous. "In an emergency, you would need an injury."

"*Need?* I'd *need* an injury?"

"The old Lanny protest. You *know* that this is the obvious, necessary, course."

The seductive charm of a little black disc. But she was right. I did know it. Once again, I was faced with the only way. If it came to a desperate choice, my fears were irrelevant. The difficulties of accomplishment were irrelevant. There was the the problem, there was my next step.

"What about Mikel?"

"You must start to move more quickly. Everything must move more quickly. It might be that you will have to miss out some of the approach steps."

"We need to know when the Final Step is going to take place."

"You must assume that it will be very soon for both of you. Move quickly. Neither of you can try to avoid the operation without raising suspicion. As a last resort, you must both be injured or ill, but that, too, would arouse suspicion. We need you both out, before this imminent operation."

"What a predicament. I'd hate to be me."

"Yes. Difficult and dangerous. But we knew that, didn't we?"

"Yes, we did. If I were to fail, it wouldn't be for the lack of effort. To use the old expression, death or glory."

"It *is* a good thing."

"I know. Well, today and tomorrow are my factory days. As soon as I'm back in school, I'll try to find a way of letting Mikel know. But in spite of the speed need, I'll still have to be very careful."

"Of course."

"Right. I'll report the day after tomorrow."

The work in the factory became even more tedious. I needed to be doing things which I was afraid of doing. Yes, I was trained, and yes, we had planned; but actually doing the things was another matter. I realised that I had been enjoying the delicately subtle approach because it was a way of deferring the moment when caution was thrust aside and I spoke plainly to Mikel. I became angry with myself. After all that I had been through before my rescue, and after all my training on the mountain, now I was being a nervous little boy.

But the State was so powerful, had so much control. Every person was a camera and a recorder; every person was a spy, looking for spies. There was less need for OGs and their bullying because people were watching themselves; not just looking for wrong behaviour, but looking for slight signs, such as mannerisms, stammers, sighing when it rained.

And I was right in the middle of it, acting a role, and preparing to enlist someone and prepare him for removal.

So, it was full speed ahead, in first gear, with my foot on the brake, and ready to leap out of the vehicle.

I didn't have to approach Mikel because he approached me. He was sent to work in the same factory. "Citizen Student Yong. I am joining you in this valuable work."

I hesitated for a moment as I tried to respond without using 'pleased' or 'glad'."

"You will find it fulfilling, as I do."

"School *and* work. And soon we shall take the Final Step."

"Yes." A short pause. "I believe the time is right."

"So do I, Citizen Yong."

A hint of a smile. At such times, such small things become immense.

I turned and walked away. The conversation had been too long, and could arouse suspicion.

We ignored each other for the rest of the day, and the next day. It was necessary, but always, I was aware of the diminishing time left.

CHAPTER NINE

Was it another example of mind-control, or one of the State's blatant insults?

"Rice and beans tonight," my assigned-mother said, almost brightly. So, a change from beans and rice.

"Very nourishing. Gymnastics tonight, Citizen Mother."

Citizen Father worked late in his office. He was a factory manager, and therefore was expected, and clearly wanted, to work late every night. That suited me. I had the strong impression that he had not chosen to be an assigned-father.

Citizen Mother replied, "That is so." Full marks for bland neutrality.

I was feeling peckish, so I enjoyed the rice and beans, and the rice pudding was tolerable as something filling.

At the end of the meal, I said, "With your permission, Citizen Mother, I shall go to my room and do my homework until it is time to leave."

"You have permission."

Groaningly mechanical. But at least life at home was calm, almost sedate. While doing the pointless, and very easy, homework, I could turn my mind to thinking about my next approach to Mikel. Decisive, definite, but subtle and perfectly secret. That was the challenge, urged on by that silently ticking clock.

I was still thinking, or trying to think, when I set off for the school. I was walking along the main, straight route, with its regular set of camera poles, its inevitable drifting discs, when something made me glance to my left. At an acute angle to the main route was a narrow lane at the back of some warehouses on one side, and factories on the other. It was the sort of mysterious passage which we didn't need to be told to avoid. It had no cameras, so it was out of bounds. One of the many rules which didn't need to be written or stated. We all *knew*.

At this end of the lane, a girl stood looking at me. Automatically, I looked at her in my peripheral vision, barely turning my head. She watched me for a couple of seconds, then turned and walked down the lane.

Reassuring myself with the excuse that I followed someone who was behaving suspiciously, I turned off the main route and entered the lane. Now that I was so close, it was very gloomy. Both the factories on the right and the warehouses on the left had blank walls, with occasional doors which were probably for receiving supplies. No windows. That suited me.

About half way along the lane, the girl glanced back at me, knocked on a warehouse door, and disappeared inside. This took the level of danger up a few notches. Following someone was safe; following someone into a large building was entirely different.

As I stood hesitating at the door, trying to raise the courage to turn the handle and enter, it opened a little way, and the girl said, "Come in. Quickly."

Hoping that this meant the good possibility, and not any of the bad possibilities, I stepped through into the light of a small torch. The door was closed behind me, and she said, "Walk to the light."

When I was close, the torch beam moved up, dazzling me, then continued up to illuminate the face of Mikel Brovnik. In the same moment, I was tense with anticipation and relieved. But in the next moment, caution set in again.

"Citizen Student Brovnik," I said. "This is an unexpected occurrence."

"It's what you want, though, isn't it?"

"Citizen Student Brovnik. Please state your business, and introduce your companions."

"Ah," he said. "I understand. Increase the light, Shala."

Two of them. Mikel, I knew. I'd seen the girl, but hadn't taken any notice of her. Still, I hesitated, afraid to step into the abyss of commitment.

"Citizen Student Yong," Mikel said with a touch of impatience. "You have been observing me for a while. I really think the time has come for us to stop being afraid, at least for a few moments."

"Citizen Student Brovnik, I regret that my part in this must be kept largely in secrecy. That is for the sake of other people, and of you, on the grounds that you can't divulge what you don't know."

"The problem with that being that the torturers probably wouldn't believe that I don't know."

"There is that. But let's leave it that I must be secretive."

"Okay. But am I correct in assuming that in broad terms, our aims are the same, or similar?"

"We believe so."

"We. Ah. Why do you believe so?"

"You have shown signs, which we have interpreted."

"Now that does make me worry. If *you've* seen signs, others probably have, too."

"That is what we fear. That is why my great caution has been in the awareness that we must move quickly."

"To do what?"

"To remove you. To recruit you. You are the first. This is a very slow beginning."

"Are you building an army?"

"We are building a country, a world. Very slowly. One at a time. What progress have you made here?"

"Very little. Just Shala and I keeping our sanity, keeping our brains working. Just being a tiny secret group helps to do that. Thinking when thinking is forbidden, communicating when private communication is forbidden; just the struggle and the discipline are our incentive. But there is no imagined end, no result for us to aim at. We just keep going from day to day."

"And you do it very well. Only a certain great mind was able to detect, and even he wasn't sure. I was sent to find out, and then to recruit."

"Will Shala be allowed to follow?"

"Yes. But patience is required. Which brings me to the need for urgency in your case."

"I have signed for the operation."

"Yes. You must leave before that happens."

"So, I leave, and, presumably, you leave. What about Shala?"

I hesitated. This was another defect in the Professor's plan. It was that too precise focus again. He had identified Mikel based on his verbal and written communications; well, of course that meant that one other at least was involved. The Professor could see one-at-a-time as an essential theory and policy; but he hadn't considered how we were to protect those who were left.

I turned to Shala. "Have you signed for the operation?"

"No. I'm a year younger than Mikel. So far, I've avoided it."

"Right. That takes away the desperate urgency. You will be removed when it is practical to do so. Mikel and I shall return, disguised, altered. In the meantime, do what I have been struggling to do: exhibit perfect obedience and conformity, in every little thing, while keeping your mind intact. You must retain, and maintain, your secret sanity."

Mikel said, "That's a lot for her to do alone."

Time for firmness. "Yes. And bear in mind, Shala, that when Mikel returns, you might not recognise him. Even if you do, he might ignore you for weeks, months. It's a recycling process. We leave, are changed, we return. With a new identity. We recruit and remove. One vast, continuous process. That is the plan. But it isn't for a revolution in the form of a rising and overthrowing the tyrant, He doesn't want that. Not yet, anyway. That leads either to failure or to a new tyranny. His aim is: remove, educate and train, return to remove. Over and over.

Shala said, "That makes sense, Mikel. You must go."

"How will it be arranged?"

"Your parents were transferred as mine were, which makes it easier. You will disappear, a presumed suicide. But the details will follow. I shall report on this vital meeting."

"We had better leave. We have been here for too long."

"Yes. I shall continue along the lane, then return to the main road, having followed a suspicious girl. Do variations on that. And until something changes, continue as we have been doing."

"Yes, Citizen Student Yong."

I smiled. "Goodbye, Citizen Student Brovnik. Goodbye, Citizen Student. . . . "

"White."

I nodded. I opened the door slightly, and peeped out. Then I squeezed through, and hurried along the lane.

CHAPTER TEN

KATINA ALMOST BRISTLED with energy when I told her of the latest development. In her usual way, she paused for a moment to pass the message on, somehow, and receive a message back.

"The Professor says that now is the crucial, and most dangerous, stage, fraught with crises. We must be very careful."

"I know," I replied, "and that is the most difficult part. I am to proceed straight ahead to the destination, but straight ahead takes me through minefields and crocodile pits."

"This is why you trained, learned, and worked so hard. This is why you endured so much. Remember your month alone in the forest, fending for yourself?"

"How could I ever forget it?"

"That was preparing you for this just as much as your history lessons, your role-playing, your attempts to become adept at computer technology. During that time in the forest, you were ill, injured, starving, in great pain, afraid. And alone."

"So a bit of State torture will be a doddle."

"Don't be obtuse. You know and understand what I'm saying."

"Yes, I know. I know. It's all been leading to this climax. And part of me relishes it. But another part of me wants to come and live in that disc with you."

I thought I detected emotion when she said, "It would be rather cramped."

I wasn't just being affectionate: it would be safer in there.

She said, "When the time comes, you will be shown how to summon me to set things going. As you know from your own rescue, perfect timing is essential."

"I'll always be amazed that you and the Professor managed it in the circumstances."

"It certainly was impressive. But again, as previously discussed, we don't want a drama this time. Mikel is to disappear, not be seen escaping."

"Understood. Well, after our long session last night before the gymnastics, for which we were all almost late, I must let things settle down for a couple of days. I must be detached, remote, and so on."

"Yes. And be alert, and suspicious of everyone and everything around you."

"Yes."

I expected her to say one of her departure phrases, such as 'report again tomorrow'. Instead, there was a pause, and then she whispered sharply, "Look out! OGs." Instantly, she disappeared. A moment later, with heavy footsteps, two OGs emerged from a bush.

As usual, their faces were hidden behind one-way visors attached to their helmets. And as usual, they did a bit of muscle flexing before pointing their guns at me, and looking round.

One said, "All right. Where is she?"

It was time for more than mere ignorance. "*What?*"

They took turns as usual. The second one said, "Your accomplice. She was talking to you. We heard you plotting."

"No," I said, very condescendingly. "What you heard was my arguing with myself about the best ways to implement State policies."

This explanation depended on their not having heard what was being said, or having heard very little of it.

"We heard a girl's voice."

"No. Just my less than entirely masculine voice when I'm excited about something."

"What was that about being suspicious of everyone and everything around you."

I gave him a puzzled look. "Don't you think I should be?"

"Don't you answer back to an Outer Guardian!"

Good: he was rattled.

"You shouldn't be talking to yourself."

I wanted to tie them in knots, but it was time for a little conformist craven humility.

I sighed. "You're right. The problem is my need to reprimand and correct myself without actually thinking. That's why I use role-playing dialogue. I didn't mean to do anything wrong."

"We shall report this as an incident."

That was good and bad. They were subsiding and about to leave, but my aberration was going to be placed on the records.

"Yes, sir."

"Where are you supposed to be?"

"At the Central Packing Factory, sir. I was a few minutes early."

"When you're a few minutes early, go and do a few minutes early work instead of talking to yourself."

"Yes, sir."

He flicked his helmeted head to show that I was to scurry off, suitably chastised and humble.

Shortly before I arrived at the factory, Katina popped down. I knew what she was going to say. "You should have gone straight into subservience, even as you explained. That was a bad mistake."

"I know."

She flew, skimmed, whatever it was, almost instantly out of sight. I took a deep reviving breath, and went into the factory.

As the reception OGs were checking me, a voice behind me said, "Citizen Student Yong. I anticipate a day of great production."

"Citizen Student Brovnik. Every day here is one of great production."

As the OGs prepared to check him, I walked on, wondering whether his transfer had been a coincidence or a plant to draw us into error. I didn't like it. I was determined to keep well away from him, unless our factory work forced us together.

There is no greater frustration than needing to talk, but not being able, or permitted, to do so, except in approved banalities. Our work did bring us often close to each other. We were both much too disciplined, and afraid, to risk any form of communication; but the next challenge was in not pointedly avoiding conversation or looking at each other. Averting one's eyes could be seen as suspicious. Why doesn't he look at his colleague when he passes the box to him for sealing? Even though there was no need to look at him, resisting a natural, careless impulse could be just what someone needed to add to *this* curious act and *that* curious act, to make a desired total.

I began to sense Mikel's frustration, and he probably sensed mine. There was no escape. We couldn't go off anywhere, perhaps to take a message, to fetch some equipment, to have a break. We were stuck in our confined area, I putting items in boxes, Mikel sealing them and putting them on a conveyor belt.

When work ended for the day, we showed no enthusiasm for leaving, just as there was no enthusiasm at the end of each day's last lesson. Placid indifference was always required. As we walked out in the crowd, I felt a note being slipped into my pocket. That was dangerous; not only the passing of the note, but the writing of it. People didn't write. It was regarded as very suspicious.

On the other hand, we had reached the point at which we needed to start taking risks.

I didn't look at the note until I was in my bedroom after tea. Even then, I did it very furtively. I couldn't be sure that there wasn't a camera in my room. It said: *My Final Step next Tuesday.*

The next morning, I loitered by one of the Katina trees. I didn't have to wait for long. I said, "Katina. I need instructions. Mikel's operation is next Tuesday. I need a definite escape plan."

"I shall verify shortly."

It was time for risks. In school, I looked at Mikel, and he said, "Citizen Student Yong, I have happy news. Final Step for me is next Tuesday."

"It is happy news, Citizen Student Brovnik. You are ready and eager to go."

"Yes. It is a wonderful thing."

We said no more, and I walked away.

The rest of the school day passed with a terrible, tedious slowness. I was eager to be doing, or at least planning and preparing; but I had to sit through hours of turgid recitations of propaganda. No matter what the subject was, it dissolved into phony maxims and aphorisms about the all-powerful, always wonderful State. I felt more bitter than usual.

I wanted to arrange our departure, and I wanted to go and not come back. At least not for a long while.

But that wasn't the agreement. I must come back, as soon as it was relatively safe to do so. I must keep coming back to do my work. Each time, a new identity; a new person to learn and become. I was bound by my conscience, and reluctant desire, to do whatever the Professor required of me.

Katina was ready for me. "That building where you had your first meeting with Mikel has stairs which go to the roof. That will be the collection point. It is gymnastics tomorrow night. As you did before, make your slight detour, Mikel to do the same, then go as quickly as you can to the roof, and wait."

"Right."

"Be careful how you tell Mikel. It must be clear, but subtle.

This is now the danger point. They might already be suspicious. Subtlety and decisiveness make a difficult combination."

"I know."

"But we have confidence in you."

That was encouraging.

It was time for me to have some, too.

CHAPTER ELEVEN

"Gymnastics tonight, Citizen Student Brovnik."

"Yes. Always a stimulating experience."

"It will be. As it was last week."

Accompanied by a strong look, I hoped that it would be sufficient. I was relieved to see understanding in his eyes.

I said, "I shall see you there."

"Yes."

It was done. We separated. It was important now to maintain the simultaneous conflicting focuses of what was going to happen tonight, and what was going to happen in the lessons, and time at home, before the great event. We had to be model students, model children, doing nothing to arouse any slight suspicion. And we had to avoid looking like two people who were trying to avoid doing anything to arouse any slight suspicion.

Occasionally, I had seen Shala, the girl from the warehouse, and she was impressing me with her detachment. I thought that she deserved to be the next recruit.

On and on went the lessons. It was important, vital, not to fidget, not to lose concentration. And to be ready, always ready, for an attack.

"Citizen Student Yong! You seem not to be interested in The Great War of Attrition!

"Citizen Teacher! I am entirely absorbed. I confess that I had mental pause for a few seconds as I contemplated the great sacrifice of our brave soldiers at The Bridge of Flowers."

"Very well, Citizen Student Yong, but do not miss any of the facts which I tell you."

A small bow of respect.

Always ready.

But there was no drifting in the rest of the lessons. A good response should be used sparingly, not be seen as an accumulation of excuses.

As I always did, I left school for the day with a show of reluctance, but I increased my speed when I saw Mikel approaching. If we spoke now, it might look as though I had been waiting for him. I hurried home, restless and excited.

"Citizen Son."

"Citizen Mother."

"Did you learn well today?"

"I did. It was all very interesting."

"Did you have tests?"

"I had one test. I had full marks."

"That is satisfactory."

"May I go up to do my homework."

"Yes. In twenty minutes, wash your hands and come down for tea."

"Yes, Citizen Mother."

I was looking forward to being away from this apartment and these parents. At such times, it almost became the most desirable part of the rescue.

I did my homework carefully, not so much working out correct things as providing the answers which were wanted and expected. As a symbolic parting meal, tea was something unrecognisable. It was a bland creamy pasta mess. I think. The only slight pleasure was in trying to identify it. And I think the pudding was the same thing with syrup. It almost made me vomit. If ever the State was defeated and overthrown, the long list of people who had deliberately been cruel to other citizens would include everyone responsible for such a disgusting meal. Yes, the contents of my bowl constituted an offence against humanity. It made me long for some beans and rice.

"Gymnastics tonight. Do I have your permission to attend?"

"Yes."

Shortly after, I was on my way. So far, it had been easy as I went through my robotic routines. But I was about to enter the danger zone. There seemed to be more discs than usual hurtling and hovering. They really did resemble flies in their irritating ways. I wondered whether one day, they would be programmed to be more aggressive, landing like flies on one's face, snapping an urgent message that one was to report immediately to a security office.

I kept adjusting my speed, trying to find a gap. Briefly, there was. I walked briskly, not visibly hurrying, into the lane, and walked at the same speed to the door of the warehouse. This time, I opened the door and walked in. As before, it was almost black.

"Citizen Student Yong."

"There are stairs," I said. "We must go to the roof."

"That's what I expected. Follow me."

I followed his voice, then his footsteps, through a door, and onto the stairs. I felt horribly trapped. Stairs are not a good place to be when being pursued, especially when the enemy is at the top and the bottom. And the darkness just added to my prickling nervousness.

I counted the flights: eleven. In spite of my physical training on the mountain, I was tired. It was probably caused by stress, and my recent meal. I was relieved when I heard Mikel fumble with the door, then open it.

When we stepped outside, Mikel said, "That first time, I checked the place, and came up here. We're the highest building around, so it's the perfect place for the removal."

"Yes. It's an excellent location, but I shan't relax until we're well away from it."

"I appreciate your efforts. And the others' efforts."

"You're welcome. They are the brains behind all this. I'm just the dogsbody."

"Much more than that. Oh."

Even I hadn't noticed the arrival of the Professor. "Lie over my knees," he said to Mikel. Quickly. And don't move. This isn't very stable."

I was reminded of my rescue, and I felt nostalgic.

"Well done, Lanny," the Professor called as the machine moved away, rising rapidly.

"Success," I said to the hovering Katina. "I'll be so happy to be back on the mountain."

"Lanny."

"Yes?"

"Don't you know what I'm going to say?"

I'd been in denial. "You don't even need to say it. I must stay, or Mikel's disappearance would look suspicious."

"That's right."

"Oh, well. Back down the stairs, and off to gymnastics."

I opened the door, and stopped, listening. "Katina," I whispered. "They're coming up the stairs." Another horror: trapped on a roof with security people coming up the only stairs.

"Same again," she said. She flew across to one of the edges. "This side. I'll put you down nearby."

This was no time to discuss. I grabbed her, and leapt out from the roof. We flew, dropped, floated, skimmed, right and left, into a narrow alleyway. I skidded and rolled, pleased to have escaped.

"Don't rush," Katina said. "You're almost at the school. No cameras pointing at this alley. You should be safe."

"Yes, but why are the security guys at the warehouse? They might know, they might want to arrest me."

"You'll have to do your best. In an emergency, I'll try to reach you. Bluff, be plausible. Be brave."

I could manage the first two; I had big doubts about the last one.

CHAPTER TWELVE

I HAD the criminal's paranoia. Every OG, every camera, every other student seemed to be watching me with special attention. Any moment now.

"Citizen Student Yong. Report to Citizen Principal immediately."

This was it. The first step on the long torture road. And after that, if there were enough of me left, the insertion of the ultimate control into my brain.

I rose, bowed to Citizen Teacher Brand, and left the room. It was a long walk to Citizen Principal's office. It must always be a long walk, even for those who are not in great trouble; but for me, it was an occasion for the dread of all that now lay before me.

I knocked on the door, and hearing 'Enter', I walked in. I wasn't surprised to see a sour-faced, rigid security official, sitting to the side.

Right, then. It was time for the performance of my life. I wouldn't go down without a fight.

"You may sit," said Citizen Principal. I noticed that the chair was farther away from his desk, closer to the security officer.

"This is Citizen Security Officer 4. He has some questions which he wishes to ask you."

I looked at the security officer as though he had come to make an exciting suggestion. Not a trace of guilt on my open and honest face.

"Citizen Student Yong. What do you know of Citizen Student Brovnik?"

"Citizen Security Officer 4. He is a student in my school, and he works in the same factory."

"You see a lot of him, then."

I let him see my couple of seconds of thought. "Citizen Security Officer 4. Only to the extent that he sometimes makes comments. For example, after I had been guilty of allowing my thoughts to drift during a lesson, for which I was reprimanded by Citizen Teacher, he commented that. . . ."

His hand snapped up. "I am not interested in mundane comments in the playground. I want to know about other things that pass between you."

"Citizen Security Officer 4. There is nothing else. I go to school to learn, and I have no reason to doubt that he does the same."

Just a very subtle shift; a slight assertiveness, fully controlled, delivered robotically, as I had done before. He didn't know it, but I was challenging him, pulling the questions out of him.

"Well, you might be very wrong about that."

"Citizen Security Officer 4. Has he committed an offence?"

"I'll ask the questions."

I gave a little bow. I liked doing that. It relieved me of having to speak or try to decide quickly what expression to assume.

"Where were you last night?"

"I went to the gymnastics. On the way, I followed a girl. It's the second time that I've done it. I suspect something. Both times, I have followed her into a lane, but she has disappeared."

There you are. All out in the open, instead of waiting for his probing. His mental script had a list of questions, and I had answered most of them, leaving him to find his place again. I was still in danger, but I was trying to control the interrogation, make him have doubts, about me, and the questions.

He scowled. "It is you who are suspicious. I am not satisfied with these answers."

The difficulty now was not to look confident, while not looking guilty. I settled for a slightly disappointed look. "I am sorry."

"Sorry for what?"

"Sorry that you are not satisfied with my answers. Perhaps I can express them differently."

"It is not the words, not in themselves, it is what they mean I don't like this deviation to follow anonymous mystery people. It sounds to me like a big lie."

"I am sorry."

"And stop being sorry, trying to wriggle out of your dilemma."

"I am sorry that my being sorry is not acceptable. I regret also that my pursuit of the suspicious girl in accordance with State Directive 493B, Section 19 is not acceptable."

Preparation is so important. It wasn't advisable to quote regulations in my defence, but this incompetent official needed to be put in his place. A tantrum was inevitable, but that merely added to his weak position in this.

He actually stood to deliver his spittle-soaked diatribe. "Don't you quote regulations at me! You are a worthless little schoolboy, and you are going to be punished. I will not tolerate insolence. And I shall report your highly unsatisfactory responses to my questions. Consider yourself under great suspicion, and to be subject to full surveillance."

I stood and bowed. "I understand, Citizen Security Officer, and I look forward with even greater enthusiasm to my forthcoming Final Step operation."

My response calmed him. "Ah. That is good." He wagged a finger at me. "Then, you will *have* to behave properly."

He turned to the Principal and said, "So, you will soon be losing a student. He will have special duties after it is done. And I see no further problem with him."

"Citizen Security Officer 4," I said, "Citizen Student Brovnik mentioned that he was going to have the operation on Tuesday. Is anything the matter with him?"

A short hesitation while he checked his mental lists for the protocol when an interrogated student asked a question. "Yes. Citizen Student Brovnik has disappeared. Did you see anything unusual in his behaviour?"

I looked mildly puzzled. "No. We spoke briefly in school yesterday. He looked perfectly normal in every respect. And he was very excited about the Final Step operation."

"Nevertheless, he has disappeared. If you think of anything, or hear of anything, notify me immediately."

"Yes, Citizen Security Officer 4."

The Principal raised an eyebrow at him. "Yes," Citizen Security Officer 4 said. "He may go."

I bowed and said, "Citizen Security Officer 4. If I see the girl again, shall I report it to you? And shall I not follow her?"

He considered this bold enquiry. "Inform me. Don't interfere with her. After the Final Step, you will be able to do the job much more efficiently."

I bowed and left.

Using the Final Step students as high-level spies, detectives, all-round snitches and sneaks, was an obvious step.

Unless I arranged my own disappearance very soon, I was going to become one.

CHAPTER THIRTEEN

"You'll need to be ill or injured," said Katina.

I disagreed. "I'll need to be taken away as part of a faultless escape plan."

"That is what we want. I was being pessimistic because it is necessary. Your selection hasn't appeared yet on the computer records, but we must be ready with the escape plan, and the alternatives to the escape plan. Hence the suggestion of illness or injury."

"Understood."

"In the meantime, do what you can. Is the girl accessible?"

"I see her in passing. I'll try."

"Good. I know that it's tempting to stay safe until your removal, but we do need as much information as you can find."

"Yes. I understand."

"At least we know there is the potential for a developing network. You can advise, help her to prepare for eventual removal."

"Slow down there. In a society in which there is hardly any conversation, and everyone and everything is watched and listened to, you're asking a lot. I'm now in a class with three Final Step students. They're like people who have been blind, and suddenly recovered their sight. They keep slowly turning and looking at me, which could mean that a security officer is looking at me. I know that security people can see what they are seeing, but I'm beginning to think that the security officers might be controlling them, too, either directly, through spoken instructions, or through some form of remote control. How should I respond? Try to ignore it? Wouldn't that look suspicious. Stare boldly back? Also suspicious. Or should I smile and wave? That's what I sometimes feel like doing. And remember that it's only a few days since my difficult conversation with the security officer at the school. Once under suspicion, always under suspicion. That's a State maxim. And it's true."

"Do your best."

"And another thing: I want my removal planned well in advance. No drama. No leaping from buildings to escape from pursuers."

"That has always been the intention. Javid Yong is to walk silently out of here, never to be seen again, a presumed suicide. Not an escape. You will disappear, and reappear as someone else. Over and over."

"I admire your confidence, but permit me to point out that the view from the mountain, and the view from up in the air, encourage one to be confident. Down here in the thick of it, not so much."

She descended and hovered very close to me. "Remember that the Professor has worked for years secretly within the computer systems in which all their plans and policies are held, even sharing policy changes and upgrades. A large part of his life has been lived in those systems which control everything that happens in the State. He does know the difficulties and the dangers. Every day, he suffers as a father would do when his son goes off to war. Never doubt that, Lanny. He asks so much of you because there is so much to do."

"No more complaining, Katina."

Feeling emotional, I looked at that small, black disc,

yearning for the girl who didn't exist except in that stupendous, tiny computer. I said, "Are you smiling, Katina?"

"If I could, I would."

"If I'm like a son to the Professor, what am I to you?"

What does it mean when a computer pauses?

"My best friend," she replied. "So take care."

During my training with the Professor and Katina, fact had been combined with fiction, though always clearly separate, so I knew from both sources what an end of term feeling was. And that's what I had now. It was careless, sloppy, and dangerous; but I was almost tingling with the thought of soon being away from all these citizens and assigned parents, and thinking twice before saying nothing.

And I felt confident. I had rescued one person, and now I could begin on another.

Shana was next.

I began the process. First, the look. Then, the cough and the look. Then, more looks. Two days passed like this, the imperceptibly delicate vibrating of the threads of my web.

After two days, she'd had enough of subtlety.

We were leaving one lesson, on our way to the next one, when she said, "Ooh," turned sharply, and jabbed her elbow into a rib or two.

With the expected restraint, I confined my cry of pain to somewhere deep within, releasing only a residual loud, deflating exhalation.

"Citizen Student Yong!" she exclaimed, her face depicting horror and shame. "I am sorry. It was an accident."

"That is understood, Citizen Student White. As we hurry to our lessons, such an accident is likely."

We needed to come quickly to the point. We had drawn attention to ourselves. But we also needed to be subtle again. "I shall be very glad when it is healed. It makes me envious to watch the gymnasts."

"I do enjoy the gymnastics. It's the under twelves tonight."

"I shall be there."

The brief look, of understanding, I hoped.

We had kept walking as we talked. It was expected, and I wanted us to stay within the crowd. Always stay in the crowd. I had already been rebuked for going my own way. Secret conversations should always be spoken openly. I was pleased that she had forced it out of me, but she really had hurt me, and possibly caused damage. She was thin, and her elbow was sharp. I hoped any watching security officers wouldn't note it as one of my weak spots.

The next lesson was Geography. This was as much about what wasn't said or shown as it was about what *was* said and shown. Although there were variations, every lesson contained the same basic information. On the world map, to right and left were west and east States; in the middle was central State, which was this one, with no countries, with their divisions and regions; only zones and districts, which were all displayed according to what was produced. There was Central-East-North Food Production, Central-East-South Machine Production; and so on, all over the Central State. There were more detailed maps, like descending satellite views, showing which food, which machines, in the zones within zones. And then there were all the percentages and other performance criteria for each zone and sub-zone.

As with so many of the school subjects, it was horrible, but interesting, especially when I had switched off from my mission onto being just another mindless student. It was one way of staying awake and relatively alert. Citizen Teachers could detect wandering attention across a crowded classroom.

Lesson after lesson, shuffle after shuffle, then home, such as it was, and my artificial family. Sometimes, the pretence reminded me of real home and family life, at least so far as it had been permitted by the State. I had been a real son, to real parents, both of whom, if still alive, were separated from me and from each other, working in an unknown zone, doing an unknown job.

I'll find you. One day. I said this so many times. My little commitment, My promise.

Tea tonight was sardines, peas and rice, followed by pastry with syrup on it. Tolerable. It would do to set me up for tonight's little adventure.

It was as I walked into my bedroom that I stopped, with a bolt of horror passing through me. All through the cautious arranging with Shana, both of us eager to meet, I had forgotten, and she had forgotten, or not been aware, that the warehouse was no longer a safe location. The security officers had recently charged up the stairs, looking for suspects. I still didn't know why, but that didn't matter just now; what did matter was that Shana was going to walk into an area which would now be scrutinised. Locations were like people: once suspected, always suspected.

And it wasn't just danger for Shana. Under interrogation, she could be the link to Mikel, who could be the link to me. She might even reveal me directly.

She had to be stopped before she arrived.

But how could I do that in full view of cameras, OGs and discs?

CHAPTER FOURTEEN

I WANTED TO RUN. I needed to run. I must arrive first. All that was needed was a small gesture to call it off. But even thinking it was merely fantasising. Any surveillance would see me doing something very suspicious. Running? Why? And it could easily be linked to Shana, who would shortly be trying to explain why she was entering that warehouse.

I didn't even know from which direction she would come. I couldn't guard both ends of the lane at the same time. Besides, we were back to the questions: why was I standing at the end of that lane when I was supposed to be on my way to gymnastics at the school?

Trying to look inconspicuous, I left the main road, and entered the lane.

I was too late.

She was standing with two OGs, and a security officer. The security officer was also in full uniform, so that was three helmeted, visored, men, looking down at her, asking difficult questions. She looked very small.

I almost stopped, almost kept going, almost collapsed under the strain of a cluster of predicaments and indecisions. She glanced in my direction, and they turned and saw me. I kept going, knowing that there was only one way out of this for me, and the great plan.

I walked firmly, purposefully towards them.

"Citizen Student!" the security officer said as I approached. "This is a surprise. It looks as though we've caught a pair."

"Citizen Security Officer," I said calmly. "You have caught one. Citizen Security Officer 4 has had my account. I have followed this girl twice before. I was instructed to report any subsequent grounds for suspicion."

The security officer moved a little from us, tapping a message.

"Bit slow," said one of the OGs. "She not only entered the lane, but went into this warehouse, which we have reason to believe is a den of plotters against the State."

I decided to make them do a bit of work. "What was in there?" I asked.

"This girl."

"No. I meant the den of plotters thing."

The other OG tapped his colleague, and said to me, "Citizen Student. You haven't been cleared yet. Stop asking questions." He paused. "And don't ask questions anyway."

The security officer came back. "Reply from Citizen Security Officer 4. He confirms that's the account you gave him. But he adds that doesn't mean you were telling the truth."

Shana now rallied to do something very clever. "Citizen Security Officer. It's because of this person following me that I have been going down this lane and hiding in the warehouse. I tried to lead him into a trap. But he never followed me into the warehouse."

Very neatly, she was confirming my account, and providing a neat explanation for herself.

One OG said, "Well, why didn't you say that at the beginning? Why wait until he's set you up for it?"

She had the further sense to attack. "Citizen Outer Guardian. Did you allow me to speak? No. You two dragged me out here, spun me around, and told me I was in a lot of trouble; and *you* told me it's a den of plotters, stood over me, and shouted your questions, while at least one of *you* was shaking me. No wonder I couldn't speak coherently."

The security officer, the man in charge, said, "You will address the OGs and me with respect, or you will be in very big trouble."

She took some big breaths to show that she was taking hold of her emotions, and said, "I am sorry, Citizen Security Officer, and Citizen Outer Guardians. You have frightened me, and I am very upset."

"So," I said, "I was following you because you looked suspicious, and you were hiding and trying to trap me because *I* looked suspicious."

"Yes."

"Citizen Security Officer, Citizen Outer Guardians, I apologise for both of us. We have allowed our enthusiasm to cloud our judgment, and have wasted your time and effort. We shall accept whatever punishment you think is appropriate."

"Citizen Student. At the very least, you may both expect a week in a house of correction. But this whole affair will have to be reported, and assessed. Take their full details."

I bowed as he walked away. Shana was overwhelmed by her effort, and the improvement in her situation. She stood blinking.

The OGs immediately dropped the formalities. Very careless. Switching on and off is dangerous. And they needed to remember their part in the great system.

"Right, names, security IDs, and addresses."

When he had tapped the information, he said, "Where are you going now?"

We both replied, "Gymnastics." I added, "To watch."

He pointed at Shana, then at one end of the lane. "You go that way." Then he pointed at me, "And you go the other way. And if we or any other OG or camera sees you two together, you'll be having a lot more than a week in a house of correction."

I was tempted to add that we'd be happy never to see each other again, just for good measure; but I decided that simple obedience would be best. OGs didn't like words coming at them.

After a little bow, I walked back down the lane, and followed the main road to the school.

After that self-protection and team protection, in a rapid double act repartee, it would have been nice to go through it together, sharing the relief, and the pleasure. But even formal greetings between us were now out of the question. The removal of Shana was going to have a long delay.

And it looked as though I was going to have another week in a house of correction.

Would punishment take priority over the Final Step? Was it all coordinated? At least my being at the house of correction might mean that I didn't keep my operation appointment.

I needed to know, urgently. If the operation could be delayed, then it would be better for the plan for me to do my week of punishment. Disappearing before the operation could be put down to extreme fear, leading to my hiding or suicide; but disappearing before the operation and the punishment for the very suspicious behaviour in the lane, would lead to some big thinking and linking, which might eventually lead to the suspicion of infiltration, and *that* was what we must avoid. For the cause, I'd do my punishment week; for me *and* the cause, I must be removed before the operation.

Yet another quandary.

CHAPTER FIFTEEN

I DON'T KNOW why I expected a notification and the opportunity for discussion. I had experience of the system. When nothing happened for two days, I was lulled into thinking that there would be no punishment, I couldn't do any more for Shana on this visit, and it was just a matter of staying out of trouble until it was time for my removal.

I suppose that's how we go through much of our lives, fooling ourselves, pretending that we can't see, hear or feel things. Like the warning signs of a disease.

Citizen Teacher Sims was excited again. "A vital part of your education is not just to read and hear about the glorious State, and to work in factories. No. You should see what is happening in other parts of this great system, in places where you might work one day. Now, today, we are going to visit one of the biggest stone quarries in Central State. I am sure you will find it of great interest. I know I shall."

He was almost informal in his enthusiasm, almost human. I could imagine him in other circumstances, a conscientious teacher being excited at the prospect of providing a new experience for his pupils.

Two other teachers were accompanying us, and an ancient

bus was waiting outside, the driver constantly tapping the accelerator to prevent the engine from stalling. This was an example of the actual, and symbolic, contradictions of the State. A class of schoolchildren, soon all to be fitted with stupendous devices to monitor and record what they said, saw and thought, boarding a museum piece of a bus which looked as though it was about to die.

Obsolete buses, bones set without anaesthetic, beans and rice the staple diet; while microscopic gadgets were inserted into people's heads to allow the State to see and hear everything. Just a matter of priorities.

The little robots were even more robotic. Sometimes, it seemed as though everything around them was of no consequence, that what they really wanted to see and hear was propaganda; the comforting flow of statistics, warnings, and endless encouragements to improve.

"Citizen Student Wong."

A Final Step watcher was speaking.

"You look calm. Are you not excited?"

"Citizen Student Kahn. I am excited, but I exercise control."

Just for a tiny moment, the tables were turned, as he decided on his response, and *I* observed *him*. He settled for, "Yes."

He turned and joined the slow boarding of the bus. I stepped forward, too, not wanting to be standing alone. I needed to mingle, not be separated and easily viewable as an outsider.

"Citizen Student Yong. Are you excited?"

I was sitting next to Citizen Student Peckitt, one of the early First Step students, and she had turned to look at me. Were they being told what to say? Had the State actually taken control of them, directing them as though they really were robots?

And was someone really looking at me now through her eyes?

"Citizen Student Peckitt. Yes, I am excited. We shall have a journey through our beautiful State, and see a State quarry where the stone for our houses and factories is dug, shaped and transported."

I was hoping that my little oration would discourage further comments by her. Long sentences generally made people nervous. They were trained to communicate with short, terse comments, with no thought required, either in speaking or in listening.

She looked away. Well, that was one way to stop the scrutiny. Big sentences, with a few big words, and watch them fold and crumple. My secret weapon.

Except that it would be suspicious, both in using language that way, and in causing their little spybots to turn away. Very frustrating for the peeping analysts.

These jolly thoughts kept me amused as the bus rolled happily along the straightness of one of the highways. Identical cars kept passing us, but at least the bus could now stay in one gear and have the benefit of its own impetus to push it along.

We passed identical towns, identical agri-silo compounds, identical steel and plastic factories with no windows, large clusters of identical tall, grey apartment blocks and offices. I pretended to find it interesting, my eyes wide and alert. That was another little axiom which had crept in during my absence. Wide eyes showed honesty of purpose, keen interest, trustworthiness; slightly lowered lids suggested lack of interest, furtiveness, introspection, even plotting.

The quarry was surprisingly close to the highway; or perhaps the highway had been designed to go close to the quarry. Transport must have been as important an issue as extraction. The bus turned onto a flat stretch of dusty road or platform, and stopped. After we left the bus, we stood and waited, students and teachers. The door of a nearby hut opened, and a man walked quickly over to us.

"Citizen Teachers! Citizen Students! Welcome to South-South-Western Stone Quarry. I am Citizen Quarry Manager Dole. I shall be your host and guide, and I hope your tour will be of great interest. But first, after your journey, I have water for you to drink, and there are washroom facilities for Citizen Students, and separate ones for Citizen Teachers. Follow me, please."

Everything apart from the actual quarrying seemed to be carried out in a series of huts, built for administrators, not for large groups of students. The result was a lot of shuffling, squeezing, sidestepping, and waiting for turns. Whenever anyone happened to look at Citizen Quarry Manager Dole, he smiled with the stoical patience of someone who must endure.

When the drinks and washroom visits were all accomplished, we were issued with hard hats, and taken out to the edge of the quarry. For the next few minutes, I stopped being aware of the other students, the teachers, even the Quarry Manager. My brain struggled to comprehend the immensity of the quarry pit. The perspectives seemed to be playing tricks with my eyes. How could there be anything this long, this wide, this deep? Rendered tiny by distance, digging machines on caterpillar tracks, accompanied by lorries, moved slowly along roads on ledges cut into the sides of the pit. I had the illusion that the city in which I lived was nothing but a children's play area, and this, *this*, was the real, the whole, world. There were no forests or fields, no rivers or seas, no valleys or mountains, except what I now saw. The world had been poisoned and carved, and hollowed, and sliced, and then removed, and taken to faraway places to be made into apartment blocks and factories and roads.

"If you will follow me, we shall go down." Citizen Quarry Manager Dole led the way to a bus at the start of one of the ledge roads. When we were all seated, he said, "We shall now go down to the bottom of the quarry, where you will see the manual work, and have a better understanding of the vastness of all this. You have stood above, and looked down; soon, you will be below, and look up."

The man was enjoying his presentation, and I appreciated it. I hoped all the observers and assessors did.

The ledges were in a long sequence of snaking turns, twenty I counted, and the journey took a long time. There was a definite ominous awareness of descent, of leaving the living world above, and going into some domain where there was only death. That was so fanciful and childish that I felt ashamed when we arrived at the bottom, and I saw all the people and activity. In this vast emptiness from which millions of tons of the world had been removed, there was a small town of workers, of buildings, streets, and machines. As we left the bus, I stubbornly shed my robot disguise long enough to say to the manager, "Citizen Quarry Manager. It's astonishing. It must be exciting for you." He glowed with pride, and the simple recognition.

He turned to a group who were using electronic slicers to reduce a slab of smooth stone to manageable blocks. They made a thick cloud of dust, but none wore a mask.

One of them, clearly supervising, glanced in our direction, and hurried over. "Citizen Quarry Manager," he said. "I am ready to take these people round."

"Citizen Section Leader will now escort you and explain."

"Please follow me," said Citizen Section Leader. I moved forward slowly, wildly conflicting emotions churning in me. I needed to be close to, and I needed to stay away from, the man who was leading us.

My father.

It was a good tour, with a lot of interesting information, well-delivered and explained, but I barely heard it, and retained virtually nothing.

I had to do something, but what? Surely, he would see through my changed appearance, recognising every feature, every nuance, as soon as I spoke.

I wanted him to recognise me, and I was afraid that he would. He mustn't. I was Javid Yong, not his son. Not yet.

When the tour ended, he asked, "Are there any questions?"

Trying to stay concealed behind other students, I called, "Do you live down here?"

"Yes. We have residential quarters on the far side, beyond those processing buildings."

"Do husbands and wives work in the same location?"

There were some turned heads and looks, and he hesitated. "There is some provision for married people."

"And do they work together?"

Another hesitation. "Some work near each other, but there is no firm arrangement. It depends on what the State requirement is."

One of the teachers stepped forward and said, "Well, I think that is quite enough on that. A satisfactory tour. Class, show your appreciation."

We all bowed.

As the crowd moved towards the bus, I paused and looked at him. He was watching me, with a puzzled expression. There must be no recognition, only his interpretation of what he saw in my eyes.

I turned and followed the others to the bus.

I had learned more about my parents' troubles from the Professor than I did from them. He could talk about the things that they were forbidden even to mention. He told me of the pressure which had been put on parents to cooperate in all things for the sake of their children. Those children whose parents opposed the State in any way, who did not conform in every way, would be deemed to be in a dangerous environment, and would be taken away. At the same time, children were encouraged to report any anti-State behaviour by their parents.

"It was a neat, circular arrangement," the Professor said. "The parents were blackmailed into obedience to protect the children that the State was turning against them. The parents were then obedient to their children, who became little representatives of the State. Even those children who didn't report their parents *might do*. There was even pressure put on the children to observe and report their parents."

I remembered those lessons, but I had merely thought of it as typical school interference, to be ignored, not part of a big plan.

I used to think that my father was a weak, defeated man, but even the strong were compelled to be weak. His fears were reinforced by the removal of mother, who had grumbled, nothing more.

My father was alive, working in dust, at the bottom of a vast pit. But he was a section leader, which meant that he wasn't the absolute dregs.

But was my mother alive? And if so, where was she?

I knew what Katina would say: *That has no relevance to the programme. That is for the far-off future.*

She was right. The Professor was right.

But it still seemed wrong.

CHAPTER SIXTEEN

THEY CAME ONE AFTERNOON, after school. A few brief words with my assigned parents, who would probably still be paid during my week away, and I was ordered out to the special van. I decided to make them do their little bit of a job properly.

"Citizen Outer Guardians. Why?" I asked.

The OG shrugged. "Don't matter. My orders are clear. I don't ask questions. Why should you?"

"Because our roles are completely different. I'm being taken to a house of correction. You're merely doing the taking."

"From your attitude, it looks like that's exactly what you need."

I did a big sigh. What was the point? Just as people were expected to behave well when they walked to the gallows or the chopping block, so I was expected to go with no fuss to my week of imprisonment. The warning that being obstructive would make things worse wouldn't have carried much weight for people going to be executed, but it did for me. There was plenty of scope for increasing my punishment. I knew that from my own painful experience.

I wondered whether *anything* had changed.

Yes. A lot. At least, for me.

"Welcome to House of Correction, Advanced Class," announced Citizen Manager 1, with a smile which was ominous.

He looked at us with almost bubbling over inner amusement. "Yes," he said. "You are quite right, Citizen Student Yong. My smile *is* ominous, because I *enjoy* inflicting pain. We all do here." He turned to a small but powerful-looking woman beside him. "Citizen Manager 3. Go and fetch my cane."

This was all staged. The cane was by a wall of the gymnasium in which we stood. When she picked it up and carried it over, I saw that it was thick but pliable. He swished it a few times, and said, "Some old remedies work well. This is one. You disobey. No writing an essay about being good. No! Cane for you. Back, bottom, legs. Shall I demonstrate? Any volunteers?"

What a comedian. Listening to his routine was additional punishment. But he looked like someone who would enjoy administering a beating. We were all wearing regulation thin jacket and trousers, giving no protection against a cane. I needed to be very careful, and that was going to be very difficult because I was in here for two weeks instead of the usual one.

The Final Step would be the following week.

So, two weeks of punishment, then *that*.

I was so absorbed that I didn't hear Citizen Manager 1 creeping towards me from an angle. He punched me on the ear, causing a flash of sickening pain, and making me stagger.

"What are you daydreaming about, Citizen Student Yong?"

"Citizen Manager 1! I am not daydreaming about anything." Not anymore.

"I have read your report. I have great suspicion of you. Whenever I see you looking like this, blank eyes, ears not working, I'll assume you're plotting something anti-State, and I'll beat it out of you. I don't mean confession. I mean I'll beat every plotting impulse out of you so you will plot no more. Do you understand, worthless Citizen Student Yong."

"I understand, Citizen Manager 1."

"Back in place."

He set off on the daily routines, the meals, the sleeping arrangements, cold showers, more punishments. It was terrifying. And yet, that old stubbornness, that pig-headed obstreperousness, was taking over.

"Citizen Manager 1!"

His head snapped round. Oh, the temerity to interrupt him. "Well, what is it, worthless one?"

"Citizen Manager 1. The injury to my ear has reduced my hearing. May I have permission to turn to my left, to hear you with my right ear?"

"No! Your injured ear is your fault. If you can't hear, you will make mistakes, and have further punishment."

I bowed. But as he started to speak, I slightly turned my head and slightly leaned forward, concentrating. Stubborn again.

It was all much as I expected, apart from the sadistic anticipation. Previously, the sadism had been confined to doing, not talking about it first.

"Now. Stand to attention." When that was done, he and his silent assistant walked past us, and we heard them leave through the gymnasium door. I knew what this was going to be.

After an hour or so, a small voice said, "Do we just stand here, then?"

Like a ventriloquist, I replied, "Yes. Don't talk."

"What?"

I let someone closer deal with the second question. I wasn't going to risk it. I wasn't going to risk anything. Someone hissed, "Don't talk."

Katina didn't know that I was in for two weeks. And I had no way of letting her know. I had to put all my concentration into surviving, alone.

I envied my father, cowed and docile, no longer treated as an enemy of the State, left to live and work at the bottom of a quarry.

I didn't know how long it was before Citizen Managers 1 and 3 returned. Two hours, three hours? He stood in front of us, and looked as though he was now going to be more direct, no comedy act.

"Citizen Student Wade. Come to the front."

When the student stood before him, Citizen Manager 1 said, "You were seen and heard to talk. So were two others, not identified."

"I'll tell you! It was Citizen Student Harrison, and . . . and someone on the front row."

"Citizen Manager 3. My cane."

She fetched the cane as before. "Turn round."

Citizen Student Wade began to cry. "I told you the other one."

"There was no deal made. Now, stop whining. Whine, and the punishment will increase."

The caning was no token gesture. He gripped the weapon with both hands, and with nimble footwork slashed it across Wade's back. The victim released a shriek which filled the gymnasium like a poison gas. Two more strokes followed. Wade collapsed, whimpering.

"Citizen Student Harrison. Come here!"

The student strode forward, trying to suggest obedience even in his walk.

"Now, I know what Citizen Student Wade said. What did you say?"

"I told him to stop talking, Citizen Manager 1."

"Why did you tell him that?"

"Because it was wrong to talk without permission, and would put him, and the rest of us, in trouble."

"Do *you* know who on the front row spoke? No punishment for you if you tell me."

"I do not know, Citizen Manager 1."

"I think a few strokes of the cane will sharpen your memory. Turn round."

With a weary sigh, I said, "Citizen Manager 1. It was I."

He almost smiled as he said, "Ah. Citizen Student Yong. I thought we'd have a confession. Now, Citizen Student Yong, what did you say?"

"When Citizen Student Wade asked were we to continue standing, my exact words were, 'Yes. Don't talk.' That seemed to be the most effective way of ensuring the continuation of our standing to attention, as you instructed."

"I asked you what you said, not why you said it."

I gave a little bow.

He looked at his watch. "Fortunately for Citizen Students Harrison and Yong, it is time for your first lesson. Think of your caning as a suspended sentence. It will be added to your punishment for any future misdemeanours."

I bowed again.

"Go to Room 4B on the next floor. Do not talk on the way."

I hadn't been caned, so I decided to accept that as something good. But it was a useful demonstration in the need to be constantly alert and mentally agile to avoid any future beatings, from anyone.

So, what was waiting for us in the innocuous-sounding Room 4B? Desks and a lecturer? More indoctrination? Or something horrible?

I wondered whether this was the essence of tyrannical control of people: this blend of certainty and uncertainty; knowing that something terrible was going to be done to you, but not knowing what, when or where. Like the terrorist torture of putting a gun to your head, but not shooting you. Not today. One day, that was certain; but not today. But each today might be the day.

There was another blinding flash of pain and shock, and I staggered against a wall.

"What are you thinking about?" screamed a small woman beside me. She was small, but I could see that she was one of those phenomena in which a tremendous mass is compressed into a small space. She emanated power. And I'd just received some of it.

I managed to say, "I was wondering what the lesson would be."

"*Wondering*? Wandering mind wondering! (Nice word play) You need a fixed mind, not a wandering mind. You need focus on all things State . . . All things duty to the State. Well, I'll teach you to focus. I'll teach your mind not to wander."

A space had immediately cleared around me, the line of shufflers dispersing into a crowd of panic. They all wanted to be well away from the violence, and well away from any possible association with me. Another simple technique of tyranny: disperse those to be controlled; never let them form into a cohesive unit. No matter whether it's a small crowd or an entire country, you must reduce them to a chaos of individual people. Their perception of themselves must always be of isolated, separated people, struggling alone in feeble impotence.

And that was *my* perception, as we carried on into the classroom, under the hawkish scrutiny of our next citizen teacher.

"I am Citizen Teacher 5!" she announced. "You will obey me in all things."

We already knew that. You don't argue with the one who has the mental power, the physical power, and complete authority over you. She had the State approval to do what she wanted with us, and it was clear that she had the willingness to do what she wanted.

And what she wanted was to cause suffering. The education of us, the training, the indoctrination, was just a by-product, the justification, the target for her career advancement.

There were no desks, tables or chairs. It seemed to be a bare room.

"Form into pairs!"

Ah, teamwork. I moved close to someone, and we almost leaned against each other, trying to convey our new existence as a pair.

"All right," she shrilled. "That will do. I said pairs, not lovers. Separate. Bit more there. One more pace." She walked round us, directing, until we all stood about arm's length from one another, as though about to do some country dancing.

"Now, enemies of the State, I'm going to make real men of you, loyal warriors of the State. Now you will learn what it is to be a man." A short, heavy pause to let the fear settle on us. "In your pairs, you will now fight each other."

There were puzzled, doubtful looks.

"FIGHT! Punch, kick, chop, strangle. The loser in each pair will be severely punished. Your choice. Winner or loser. Winner will have a chocolate biscuit, loser will be caned. Your choice."

There were still some hesitations. I heard a couple of punches, followed by a couple of 'ows'. But I understood. This was reinforcing our solitary individual status, in which survival was essential, and the obstacle to our survival was, always, the next person.

I gave my partner an apologetic look, and punched him in the throat, the nose, the chin, the throat again, trying to kill him solely in order to be the victor, and to end this horror.

I had even been trained for this. I had learned to switch between my personalities, my disguises, in order to survive. If I didn't survive, what would happen to the great plan?

But on a lower, selfish level, I simply didn't want to be caned. I preferred the horror of inflicting pain to the horror of receiving it.

My partner crumpled. Some enemy of the State! He was just someone who had made a mistake, as defined by those who wanted to instil fear and hatred in everyone.

Having been violent, I now felt sick as I listened to the horrifying sounds of violence.

How quickly the simulated hatred became real hatred.

Where there was equal fear, equal hatred, equal physical similarity, the fighting went on for a long time, as measured by someone who was desperate for it to end. It was probably minutes.

Eventually, the sounds of violence were replaced by groans and panting.

Citizen Teacher 5, strode amongst us, saying nothing, until she stopped at one of those standing, and punched him. "Hit me back!" she cried.

He started to retreat, shaking his head. "No, no."

"Hit me!" she cried, over and over, punching him as he retreated, bumping into the standing people, tripping over the prone ones.

"HIT ME!"

Provoked into a mist of unconscious terror, he swung his fist at her. She stopped it with her hand, and spoke quickly into her link "Attack on teacher in Room 4B. Immediate arrest."

Seconds later, two OGs entered in their usual noisy way, went to where her finger was pointing, and dragged the weeping boy out of the room.

"That was the second lesson," she announced. "You may attack and destroy anyone on the command of the State, but you will never oppose the State in any circumstance. I am the State."

There was another lesson: the State will often give you two choices, both wrong, and make you pick one.

Once again, my suppressed real me couldn't resist speaking when I should have been silent.

"Citizen Teacher 5. What will happen to him?"

She stared at me. "You dare to ask a question, which is not even anything to do with the lesson?"

"Citizen Teacher 5, I intended no disrespect. But if you had chosen me instead of him, I suspect that in my weakness, I, too would have failed."

She walked slowly over and stood in front of me. I expected

to be punched or kicked. Instead, I thought I saw a slight trace of amusement in her hard, cold features.

"Citizen Student Yong," she said. "There will be plenty of other opportunities for you to fail. Then you will find out."

In the limited space between us, I managed to bow without looking as though I was trying to attack her.

CHAPTER SEVENTEEN

AFTER THE INSULTS and the violence, the day improved. It was the cruel, then kind, approach; with, of course, a return to cruelty at some point. But this day became almost pleasant. We had an indoctrination lecture, followed by some chanting, lunch of rice and mushrooms, a 'history' lecture, and then, to everyone's surprise, a film. It was predictable, inevitable, about the brave few State loyalists against the rampaging hordes of capitalists, consisting as always of an incongruous mixture of the blond and stupid, and the dark, long-nosed and cunning.

But it was better than being beaten or humiliated.

The next day, I began to understand that this was no mere house of correction: this was a very large compound, constructed more like a residential sports and conference centre. I already knew that the State was very happy to occupy houses and centres like this which had been built by the evil capitalists. They saw it as a splendidly appropriate irony.

"Today," announced Citizen Teacher 7, "we have swimming. Very good for body and mind, swimming."

A small voice made a little joke. "Damn, I didn't bring my swimming trunks."

Citizen Teacher 7 stopped. "Ah," he said, "we have someone

who likes jokes. Tell me, Citizen Student Hall, do you like doing high dives?"

I felt a cold doubt about this swimming session.

No answer was required. Citizen Teacher 7 was already walking away.

When we were changed, we lined up along the side of the pool, at the deep end, in the shadow of an ominous tower of three diving boards at different heights. Citizen Teacher 7 looked at us all with a pleasant little smile. "Why are you all looking so worried? You have swum before."

There were several cries of 'Citizen Teacher 7! I can't swim."

"Oh, well," he said softly. "You'll soon learn. Simple choice: swim or drown. Right, in you go, all of you, and enjoy your swim."

Leaving those who couldn't swim to look after themselves, we jumped into the water.

There were gasps and wails of anguish. The temperature of the water had been deliberately reduced to an unbearable iciness.

"Swim!" we heard, "Warm up with with swim!"

I didn't care what the order was. All I wanted was to be out of this water before my circulation system closed down. Now, he was bounding with excitement, "Hey, hey. You forget your drowning colleagues. I pushed them in, you bring them out."

As I turned back, I gave him a venomous look. That was a stupid and dangerous thing to do, but it was one of those spontaneous moments when all other considerations are pushed aside by pure emotion. The drowners were making things more difficult for everyone, including themselves, by believing they were sinking, and by thrashing around with their arms and legs, making it almost impossible to reach them, let alone take hold of them.

I tried to swim under the flailing arms of one. His immediate response was to wrap his legs tightly round my head and neck, holding me under the water. Faced with a race between freezing to death and drowning, I managed to push my chin down and bit one his legs very hard. There was a slight movement, and I pulled my head away. Back on the surface, I grabbed a flailing arm and pulled, trying to swim with a sideways stroke. When I reached the side, I let go. I was too weak to pull him out, and I needed to drag myself out.

I was trembling with the cold, even struggling to breathe, and I shook my head when Mr Jocular said, "You left him behind in the water."

He snapped, "Pull him out, or you'll be a murderer!"

I actually snarled, with rage and effort, as I twisted round, grabbed an arm and pulled the feeble body out of the water.

"Right. All out, I see," Citizen Teacher 7 called. "Now, you need to warm up. Six laps of the pool. Be careful, or you'll slip." And he laughed.

Running was good advice, in other circumstances, but I was so cold, I thought my legs were going to shatter like two icicles. And even inside, the cold air was searing my lungs. I limped along as well as I could, only vaguely aware of the number of laps. I was just struggling along, putting one foot in front of the other, needing to be warm, but feeling even more cold.

"Okay. Stop."

When I slowly braked, interrupting my momentum, my legs almost gave way. I bent over, with my hands on my knees, needing to vomit, but dreading the prospect of wrenching my weak body.

"Now, where is the joker? Come on, joker. Don't be modest. I like jokes. Here's mine. You go to the top diving board and dive in. Not jump. Dive."

"I can't."

"You can. First lesson today. I'll make high-divers of you all."

So, that was it. We were all going to be put through this. From the top board, dive, not jump, into the icy water.

I had never dived. I had no idea. It had not been included in my mountain training. Even the Professor hadn't anticipated this one.

The joker was making a big fuss, pleading. He should have learned by now that there is no point; you might as well just go and do whatever it is. You had to do it anyway, why add to it? He was now receiving slaps all over his body. They reverberated and echoed all round the high-domed swimming pool. The joker stood, weeping, taking the slaps rather than go up there, and back down here, by the shortest possible route.

Citizen Teacher 7 took a short break from slapping to ask, "Any volunteers to show this coward how it's done?"

I stepped forward. I didn't want to stand here watching and waiting while they all went through the dives. If I had to do, then let's do it.

"You dived before, Citizen Student Yong?"

"Citizen Teacher 7, no, I have never dived before, and I don't want to do it now. But no point in putting it off."

He nodded. "Then, go and do it, Citizen Student Yong. Show us what you can do."

For anyone who has ever done anything like this, the determination to do a dive is something which weakens with every step up the ladder. Just going up the ladder isn't pleasant; the prospect of taking the short route back makes it many times worse. There were three diving boards, and I was going to the top one. And coming down was not to be a jump, tucking myself into a ball. No, I was supposed to launch myself into space with my arms spread and my torso presented like a sacrificial offering to the hard, cold water beneath.

It would be hard on impact. I was sure of that.

I walked slowly over the slightly vibrating diving board, and looked over. Everyone looked very far away, and the pool looked like the sort of thing that I could easily miss if a breeze caught me. A daft thought, except that it did feel pretty draughty up there..

Next thing to ponder: should I bounce and spring into my dive, or tuck my toes over the edge, lean forward and just go straight down. That one. The second one. Bouncing just increased the potential for things going wrong. And leaning forward slightly reduced the distance to the pool.

There was no way out of this. Do it, and then it's done. If you're going to shatter on impact, or crack your skull and break your neck on the bottom of the pool, delaying won't change that.

I tucked, and leaned, and pushed off into space.

For a quarter of a second, I was graceful, but my body began to tilt, my legs and arms decided to separate and have no part in a group effort, and the tilt turned into a slow somersault. The details of my hitting the water were lost in the smacking, bubbling, deafening, descent to the bottom of the pool, which I touched lightly, followed by the desperate need to rise back through the bubbling tumult. It took much too long, and in my panic, I was almost suffocating. But suddenly, I burst through into light and air, becoming aware that I had done it, and survived, and was rapidly returning to the frozen condition.

As I struggled out of the water, I heard, "Interesting style. Who's next?"

I gasped, "Citizen Teacher 7. Permission is requested to do more laps of the pool."

"Permission is granted, Citizen Student Yong."

A feeling of triumph warmed me as I ran round the pool, enjoying watching the reluctant students being slapped and pushed to the ladder. I was feeling smug, too. The next one hit the water when I was on my third circuit. He made the water sound like shattering glass. Halfway round my fourth circuit, I was summoned. "Citizen Student Yong. Citizen Student Patel is taking a long time coming to the surface. You are instructed to go down to assist him."

Was I ever going to be warm again?

Was being chosen to do the rescue a good thing?

In I went, and down I went. I opened my eyes, which instantly prickled. I saw the blurred outline of Patel, floating near the bottom. At least, he wasn't waving his arms. He was well beyond that. I grabbed him and tried to raise him, but he was now very heavy. I pushed sideways towards the side of the pool, but I had to release him and go up for more air. Back down, I tried to go underneath, safe from clenching legs, and push, but I wasn't strong enough. I tried to raise him from the side, but I couldn't do it. I broke the surface, panted, then called, "Citizen Teacher 7. I need assistance. He's a dead weight. And he might be dead."

Two students were told to assist, and I pushed, and they pulled, until the body was on the side of the pool. Citizen Teacher 7 prodded him with a foot. "Yes. Looks dead. These things happen. All part of learning. Stand by, Citizen Student Yong. You might be needed again."

CHAPTER EIGHTEEN

Two more rescues, and three more circuits, and in spite of my mountain training, I went into collapse, with hot and cold shivers, congestions, and a pair of legs which wouldn't support me. Even the callous sadists accepted that I was justifiably ill. There were no hospital facilities, but I was put in a 'recovery ward', really just a quiet place, where I could rest, and eat my meals in peace. I almost enjoyed it.

When Citizen Manager 1 visited, I knew it wasn't concern for my welfare. He didn't want the schedule disrupted.

"It is vital that you participate fully in your punishment and re-education programme."

"Citizen Manager 1. I am sorry to have missed anything of importance. Perhaps I can extend my stay here."

Another almost-smile. "The schedule has been, hmm, a little revised to enable you to recover while not missing the most important parts of the programme."

"Thank you, Citizen Manager 1." So considerate.

"So, the group sessions of lectures, films, were taken out of their programme slots and arranged together, making an easy couple of days for your colleagues, and a more challenging few days when you return. It is of course unfortunate that you have

missed some of the programme, but there will be other reinforcement opportunities before the finish."

This was firmly terminating my nice couple of recovery days.
I tried very hard to look pleased. "Thank you again. I would like
to be as close to perfect as possible by the time I leave here."

Did he detect the presence of a master flanneller? Someone
who could maintain a look of rigid innocence while emitting
blatant, fawning lies?

Or did he see a tick for success for Citizen Manager 1?

He said, "Of course. And we shall do our best. First lesson
tomorrow is in 12A."

I did my best to bow while lying in bed, and received a nod
of acknowledgment.

I lay back, and forced my tired brain to go to work on the
problem of improving my reputation while avoiding the Final
Step operation.

With a final effort of desperation, I gripped the rope and pulled.
I spoke loud to myself: "Pull! You can do it! You can do
anything! Will power. You are strong!"

The combination of body and mind failed, and I slid down
the rope, burning my hands and thighs during the short descent
to the waiting cane.

The blow was hotter than fire, and paralysed every bit of me.
I pulled on the rope simply in an effort to reduce the pain. Then,
I growled, snarled, gurgled and even let go some foul language as
I pulled myself inch by inch up that prickling rigidity of rope.
By the time I was two thirds of the way up, I was emitting only a
repetitive execration. If the sadists below didn't like it, that was
quite another matter. I had complete focus on reaching the top
of the rope.

I still cursed when my hand reached the brass hoop at the
top of the rope. Even in triumph, I couldn't switch to elation

from my teeth-gritted aggression. And I realised that after doing the impossible, now I didn't know how to go down. I couldn't use the same aggression to go down; I mustn't slide down, causing severe burns; I mustn't let go. A different sort of paralysis set in. I was rapidly becoming weak, and I didn't know what to do.

It would have to be more aggression. I transferred my hatred of the teachers into my hands and legs, and began to snarl and curse again. By the time that I reached the bottom, I was doing a rhythmical grunt, and at the slightest provocation, I was ready to tear the teacher to bits.

"That is right, Citizen Student Yong. You may rest."

Ferocious anger was instantly replaced by joy and gratitude. Now I wanted to hug her. I was approved and rewarded.

And *this*, I realised with a shock, was the State's deliberate, and very successful, manipulation of me. Over and over, it was the same thing: through gruelling exercise and pain, push me to the brink of murder, then take me softly into the place of reward and gratitude.

Running, wrestling, more cold swimming and diving, the cane administered for every failure, alternating with films and lectures; a constant reinforcing of the brutal power and comforting protection of the State, merging together, so that eventually the pain and the relief from pain became two parts of the same thing, which was a thing to enjoy and love.

And always the simple message: submit, to all of it.

Gradually, like army recruits, we all improved. The complaining stopped, there was no more whimpering, and pleading, all effort went into doing what was required. On the mountain, I could acquire strength, and survival and endurance skills, but not wrestling skills. But with the cane being swished nearby, I became stronger and more flexible in my movements. And I cheated. Every little jab, poke or grip that would give me a moment's advantage, was acceptable to me. Citizen Manager 7 did shout at me a couple of times, but I didn't care. The damage had been done. That moment of distraction had opened a door. And as for skulduggery, was the State going to object? This was all about winning the duel, every duel; here, school, office, factory; always winning the duel with every other person, every one of whom was my enemy, even as we were all loyal brothers and sisters in the State.

"Well, Citizen Student Yong, what have you learned from your training course here?"

"That physical and mental suffering, and physical and mental pleasure, are the same thing in the acceptance of the State."

There was a very brief pause, then a nod. That was all. My answer was right, but perhaps more right than he expected, or wanted.

No-one else put it so well, but with some encouragement, they all managed to deliver a version of what I had said. Some even repeated what I had said. All received the acknowledgment of a nod.

"It is clear," said Citizen Manager 1, "that you have all benefited from your training, and will be model students on your return to normal society. Your records will show that you have all completed this course.

We were led out to the vans and taken to school for the afternoon lessons. I entered the classroom feeling like a returning hero.

"Excuse me, Citizen Teacher. I have completed my House of Correction training, and have been instructed to continue with my lessons."

"Ah." The one small word conveyed interest and satisfaction. "No, don't go to your place yet. I think it will be of benefit to the class to have a brief summary of what you did, and what you learned."

What was I? Returned hero? Black sheep back in the fold? Model student? Well, there was nothing for it but to do it, and I did. In some style. I was like two people combining to provide my account. I was an inspired actor spouting the rubbish that the State poured out incessantly; and I was the converted acolyte, meaning every word that I said, about the power and the protection of the State. I went through in detail what we had done on the course, and the corresponding benefits. I even finished with a little joke: "While I don't recommend your attendance at a House of Correction, I do recommend the contents of my training there."

The class looked nervously at Citizen Teacher Holt. He gave a little grunt, a nod, and a slight elongating of the lips to indicate that the joke was permitted and approved. The class relaxed, and smiled.

In turn, I was pleased. I wanted to be approved. I concentrated through the long lesson, a double one to finish the day, and didn't miss any opportunity of offering an answer to Citizen Teacher's questions.

I was still feeling exhilarated when school finished, and I walked out through the gate. Off to my left, I saw Shana, just as she happened to turn and see me. We both tried to convey though momentary blank looks that we understood. Then, we both looked away.

"Be careful, Citizen Student Javid Yong."

The voice was behind me. A familiar voice, except for the new cold sharpness.

I glanced round, trying to do it casually, trying to keep my face partly turned away.

"Citizen Student Plenty," I said, forcing my voice to be steady and clear, but too afraid to look into her eyes.

"Citizen Student Yong. Returning from a House of Correction with a new enthusiasm does not wipe clean your slate filled with misdemeanours. You do too much looking at people. These things are noticed."

I tried to think of something neutral but acceptable. "Citizen Student Plenty. My new enthusiasm made me careless. I regret the error."

"Citizen Student Yong. It is a frequent error. This has been noticed, as has your association with people who are also under suspicion. I advise you to be very careful."

"Citizen Student Plenty. I shall take your advice."

That was the end of the conversation. She turned sharply, and walked back though the school gate. I walked home with a seething tumult of conflicting thoughts and emotions which not even the blandness of beans and rice could calm.

CHAPTER NINETEEN

"You had a rough time," Katina said.

"Yes, I did. And the Final Step is next Thursday. It is time for you and the Professor to focus on my escape plan. I have done all that I can for this visit. I know that one recruit isn't much, but I was close to a second, and, well, we knew it was going to be a slow start, and now it's time to protect your principal asset. Mikel might be better than I am, but I've had two years of intensive training. And my previous experience."

"It makes you sound a bit like a thing, but you will always be our principal asset."

"Thank you. Now take good care of me."

"We shall. The Professor has been planning. As soon as we know, we'll tell you."

I thought that a reminder was called for. "Next Thursday, Katina; and today is Friday."

"Your rescue is his top priority."

That sounded a bit formal, and I told her. "Sorry," she said. "I just wanted to reassure you that you are our first concern."

"Thanks. Well, apart from general observation, I intend to be a perfect student for the next week, staying well away from anything resembling trouble."

"That plan is definitely agreed."

From that point, I walked everywhere in a stern march, head up, eyes staring straight ahead. I saw no lanes, no potential meeting or hiding places; I barely even saw the lurking OGs. Elika was the official model student, but for my last week, I was going to be pretty close to it. Some of the citizen teachers looked nervous as I stared at them, all intense concentration and focus on every word. Even my movements were carried out with mechanical precision.

And a vital part of being a model student was not exchanging so much as a glance with Citizen Student Shana White. I didn't avoid her: I didn't see her. I saw through her. She did not exist, other than as an inconsequential transparency, in common with everyone else, but particularly so.

One day passed safely, then another, and another; and I was almost there.

Another monthly lecture provided an opportunity for a big anonymous mingling, using up some more time, another opportunity for standing and staring into blankness.

As usual, I approached the assembly hall with deliberate slowness in order to avoid the discomfort and strain of sitting, and in order to have most people in front of me, and a few similar stragglers at the side, but no-one behind.

There were more people than usual at the back, annoyingly restless, as they shuffled about, presumably trying to find a particularly acceptable vantage spot. Being already in position, and satisfied with it, I had to restrain myself from becoming irritated. Don't even emanate annoyance, I told myself, in case someone detects it.

I must be perfect.

Someone bumped against me.

The immediate apology would have made me suspicious; the voice removed any doubt.

The slight touch of a hand at my hip told me that I was about to be dragged into danger again. Exactly what I didn't want. I was tempted to hurry after her and slip the note into her pocket, perhaps with a whispered *Not now*. I glanced round, not even wanting to do that, but she had disappeared.

She could have been right behind me, but I wasn't going to look. I was going to stare at the lecturer. I was going to be thoroughly absorbed. I was going to stay thoroughly absorbed. I wasn't going to read the note until I was safely back on the mountain.

I had heard or read of stolen money seeming to burn a hole in a thief's pocket. That's what the note was doing in mine. Someone might have seen her putting it into my pocket. Someone might be counting the minutes of my not taking it to the nearest security officer.

"No countries," droned the lecturer, "no nationalities, no religions; only the State. World State. Universe State. Eastern State, Western State, Central State. All State. All one people, all controlling themselves, all entirely loyal to the State."

I had become hypersensitive, and could feel the note rubbing through my jacket and against my skin. I could feel it moving about in my pocket, surely making suspicious ripples. I could feel its weight. I could almost hear the words, demanding my presence, my commitment to treason.

I didn't want it!

I just wanted to go home.

Detestable note, silently screaming *Read me!*

Surrounded by hundreds of people, I was utterly alone.

And being conspicuously alone was dangerous.

Always alone, never alone.

For the rest of the day, I tried to concentrate on the lessons, and tried not to look as though I were trying to conceal a distraction.

Just the usual State complications, but at a very bad time.

It wasn't until I had eaten my tea at home, and gone to my bedroom, that I unfolded the piece of paper.

Meet me, 6, Poster Class.

This was an absurd risk after what had happened. It was essential that we stay well away from each other. I understood her choice. Poster Class was always chaotic and noisy, with drawings, paintings, long lengths of poster material, and all the other stationery items. And a lot of children indulged in permitted, and encouraged, excitement. Posters appealed to children.

But it was still a very bad choice. Anywhere was a very bad choice.

I looked at the time. It was nearly six o'clock. Hadn't she allowed for the necessary delay in reading the message? This was all very sloppy.

"Citizen Mother. I forgot my intention to attend Poster Class this evening. Have I your permission?"

"Citizen Son. You should not forget things. Do not do it again. Yes, you have permission."

I walked quickly towards the school, but trying not look as though I was hurrying. Being late was an excellent reason, but being stopped would involve a session of questions and answers with an OG, drawing attention to myself, and causing further delay.

I arrived a couple of minutes after it started. There was already a lively crowd, bustling about. As I hesitated by the door, Citizen Teacher looked at me.

Shana looked at me.

They both glanced to their right. A door opened, and two security officers walked out, heading straight for me. I recognised Citizen Security Officer 4. He smiled grimly and said, "You walked straight into our little trap. This time, there'll be no talking your way out of it.

CHAPTER TWENTY

EVEN IN THE moment of horror when the security officers appeared, my mind had worked quickly. I had an answer ready to challenge the accusation when it came. But it would be kept until it was the best time, or necessary.

In all the occasions when I had been in trouble, I hadn't actually been brought in as a suspect. At the security station, I was passed over to two internal officers, and taken to an interrogation room. There was the expected one small table and two chairs.

Citizen Security Officer 4 said, "Sit."

All the time since the first officers appeared, I had been looking calm and thoughtful. Now, I slightly tilted my head, as though considering his command to sit.

But I sat. He sat opposite, frowning.

"Citizen Student Yong. You have been under suspicion for some time, but have previously talked your way out of trouble. But we suspected, so we watched, and listened, and planned. A trap was set, and you walked into it."

He looked at me with a glint of triumph. I sat back and rubbed my chin.

He didn't like that. "Well," he said. "Anything to say?"

Leaning forward, I said, "Citizen Security Officer 4. Yes, I have something to say, which should clear up your little problem."

This way of talking to him was against my better judgment, and against the advice from Katina. But in this predicament, it the only way in which I could keep myself strong and confident, which I needed to be.

Ignoring his darkening scowl, I said, "I received a note from Shana White, the girl who had previously given me, and you, cause to suspect her. She requested my presence at six o'clock at the Poster Class, which I had attended only once before, when she wasn't there. Suspecting illegality and treason, I did as she requested, intending to confirm my suspicions. As you know, I didn't have the chance to do that because you intercepted me. I don't know what is going on with you and this girl, but so far as my intentions are concerned, you have misunderstood. Again."

He hissed up his nose and his darkly frowning face changed to thundery.

"You dare talk to me like that? You expect me to believe your feeble attempt to squirm out of this?"

"Citizen Security Officer 4. It is not a feeble attempt. It is the truth. And no, actually, I don't expect you to believe what I have said. However, I assume that later, I shall be discussing this with a higher authority, and that will be the right time to state again what I have just told you."

"And that higher authority won't believe you either."

Instead of arguing, I said, "Citizen Security Officer 4, when I recently encountered Citizen Shana White with two Outer Guardians and another security officer, she was in trouble, and about to be arrested. I was not convinced of her innocence, and saw this evening as an excellent opportunity to continue my attempts to investigate her. But now, it appears that she is working with you. The quality of your attempt to trap me suggests that it was her idea. Is that so?"

I was deliberately going too far. I had to take the risk. I had to break, or at least crack, his power over me. It would make him angry, and might bring early punishment, but I had to stem that flow of superiority.

He gave me a smile which showed that I had failed. He pressed a button, and seconds later, two security officers of the OG variety entered. He looked up at them and said, "This thing needs an ice and fire." To me, he said, "I believe you need to be prepared for your formal interrogation. To, er, put you in the mood to cooperate and be suitably subservient."

He flicked me away with contempt, and I was grabbed from behind, and dragged away with no opportunity to try the walking method. I was dragged along corridors, up stairs, down stairs, along a dark passage, and into a room of blinding white light. They released me to fall on the tiled floor, but I quickly stood as they put on dark glasses. They turned to look at me as though they had just become aware of my presence.

"Did we tell you to stand?"

"No. But you didn't tell me not to."

I already had my arms crossed to protect my solar plexus, but the blow knocked me off my feet. I was dragged across the floor to a pool sunk in the floor. I knew what was in there before they flung me in. More ice-cold water. At least my house of correction training had given me some experience. Of course it was horrible, but not as bad as it could have been. Trying to resist the cold, and to show my disdain, I swam about as well as I could in the cold, in wet clothes, and in a small pool. I even ducked my head under occasionally. I thought of inviting them in, but when I looked up, they weren't there. I swam to the side, and started to pull myself out.

"Where d'you think you're going?"

"Out."

"No, you don't. You stay in until we tell you to come out. And that won't be for a while."

I let go of the side and slid back into the water. I tried swimming again, but my body was stiffening with the cold, and I was close to losing consciousness. As though I was coming round from a drugged dream, I heard one of them calling, "Hey. Come out now. We don't want you dead yet. There's a lot more fun ahead for you."

I floated over to the side, but didn't have the strength to climb out. They pulled me out, and dragged me again. I was forced down into a chair, and tired tightly. They pushed the chair forward, and opened the door of an incinerator, leaping out of the way, leaving me to have the full heat. After the cold immersion, the pain was unbearable, and I screamed. Throwing myself back, I tipped the chair over, barely noticing when my head hit the hard floor. I wriggled and squirmed, trying to put even the smallest distance between me and that intense heat. I heard them laughing, and I heard the incinerator door clang shut. But I still felt as though I was on fire.

"Still feeling the heat?" he laughed. "We'd better cool you down."

I begged them not to, making them laugh more as they threw me back into the icy water.

I became aware that Citizen Security Officer 4 was speaking to me.

"I said, you're not so perky now, are you?"

I didn't bother to reply. Let him gloat. I was busy with the searing, prickling pain all over my external body, and the chaos of different pains within. I had lost count of the times they had put me in the icy water, and in front of the incinerator. Eventually, I stopped being aware long before I fainted.

"Well," he was saying, "this will cheer you up. It has been pointed out that with your Final Step in three days, it is better to have you fit for it."

"Thanks to you, that isn't likely."

He waved a dismissive hand. "No matter. It's all learning, all part of the process. We expect to lose a few on the way."

"Lose?"

"Deaths, and, well, other effects."

He clapped his hands. "So, my young troublemaker, prepare for a couple of easy days for recovery, and then the big one. And after that, all being well, your troubles will be over."

I was raised carefully onto a trolley, with Citizen Security Officer 4 muttering instructions to be careful. I was taken to a room with a bed. He asked would I like a bath, and thought it was hilarious. But I was allowed a lot of ointment, then put into a soft cotton gown and laid between clean sheets. I groaned because even that was painful, the movements and the touch of the sheets.

One more pain: a needle was stuck in my arm. "To help you to sleep," he said. "So important for your recovery."

"Did you torture Shana?"

"We didn't need to. She was always working for the State."

That was a big lie. "Give her my regards, and tell her no hard feelings."

The grey mist of sleep slipped over me as he rose and walked away.

I woke slowly, knowing that things were going badly, but deferring any thoughts about them. I was comfortable and very tired. Problems could wait.

Someone was talking. "You will stay here until you are well enough for your operation. We expect that to be by the due date. Otherwise, a special arrangement will be made for as soon as possible after that time."

I opened my eyes and looked at her. "Hello," I said, drowsily informal. Who are you?"

"That is not the way to address me."

Citizen whatever, I apologise. Please inform me of your title, in order that I may do this properly."

"I am Citizen Head of Health Development."

I murmured, "That's a big one," and went back to sleep.

But not for long. I was being shaken awake. This time, I was unguardedly irritable. "If you want me to recover for the operation, I suggest you stop making me wake up."

I focused and added, "Citizen Head of Health Development."

"You are recovering well. All you have is some damage to your skin, which is not relevant to the Final Step procedure. You will now have a short presentation on what to expect on Thursday. Citizen Student Plenty will do this."

Conflicting emotions swirled through me. What a cruel concluding irony. Instead of one day coming back to rescue her, I was going to join her in the absolute loss of all privacy and control.

Citizen Head of Health Development walked out, the door swung behind her, and as it swung back, Elika walked into the room. She stood at the end of my bed, and said, "Good morning, Citizen Student Yong. Are you looking forward to the Final Step?"

"Yes, Citizen Student Plenty. Ever since I listened to your presentation to my class, I have waited impatiently for it to happen."

"That is satisfactory. I advise that you accept all offers of sedatives between now and Thursday. It helps to be relaxed, giving not even slight, unconscious resistance. You will be awake for the procedure. That is necessary. But of course, you will have some anaesthetic."

"*Some*? I'll want a bucketful."

"It is necessary to keep you conscious, but there will be only minimal pain. There will also be some discomfort, and inevitably a strange feeling as the insertion is carried out."

"You aren't selling this well."

"It is my duty to tell you the truth. Otherwise, there could be an excessive reaction."

She looked to her right, and said, "You might benefit from some fresh air. This is one of those old buildings in which the windows can be opened. I shall open yours a little. But don't even think about trying to escape. You are on the fourteenth floor. The only way out, short of suicide would be to fly."

She walked to the side of the bed, leaned over me, and said contemptuously, "Do you know how to fly?"

Without waiting for the answer which I couldn't provide, she walked back to the end of the bed. "I thought so," she said, still sounding contemptuous. "I trust that I have made you feel much better about what is going to happen."

She walked stiffly out of the room, making the net curtain move slightly in the breeze.

I lay back, my mind an even bigger mess of chaotic confusions, as I fondled the thing that she had slipped into my hand.

A small black disc.

CHAPTER TWENTY-ONE

WE LEFT AS SOON as it was dark. I made a quick bundle of my clothes, and we performed the familiar routine, though higher than from the top of the warehouse. I landed rather heavily, and the rolling set off my surface wounds.

"The Professor will be here soon," Katina said. "We couldn't be precise about timings."

I sat up and said, "What's going on?"

"Your rescue, as planned."

"Yes, but the plan had gone all wrong. I was captured, tortured and trapped on the fourteenth floor, with no hope of escape before my Final Step operation."

"But here you are."

"How can a minicomputer be mischievous?"

"When she constantly improves herself," Katina said.

"Back to my question then. What's going on?"

"You did quite the wrong thing in rushing off in response to that note. Because of that, the whole programme almost failed. We needed some good luck. And we had it, from the least expected source. I was flying around searching, trying to detect your presence. . . ."

"For which the requested alarm would have been very useful."

"Which they would have found and removed long ago, dangerously compromising the programme."

"Okay. I'm expendable. Carry on."

"I was flying around, very carefully, because the State's discs fly at night, too, when I became aware of something strange. Someone was standing in the street, looking at me, looking *for* me. I went a little lower, and I heard her call, in a loud whisper, 'Is it you? Help me.' I went down, and hovered nearby, still very cautious, out of sight. I asked what she wanted. 'Lanny's in trouble,' she said. 'Lanny?' I repeated. 'Oh, don't you think I know my friend?' she said. 'He's been trapped and tortured, and he's going to have the Final Step on Thursday, and you're the only one who can save him.' I said, 'Do you mean the Final Step that you had?'

"She gasped or sighed. Perhaps both. 'Oh, yes. Of course. No. It didn't work. Well, it did, but after a couple of weeks, it had a terrible effect on me. I was driven mad by screechings and shriekings in my head. It quickly became worse. I began to bang my head against walls and doors, even the ground. I hit my head with pieces of hard plastic and stones. It kept becoming worse. I staggered about, with no awareness, and no balance, or even clear vision. I fell into the river, and not in the swimming way. I was drowning, choking, swallowing the filth, somehow not caring, just wanting to stop the noises and vibrations. But as I flailed about, I hit the side in the same moment that I realised it had all stopped. I pulled myself out, and lay on the bank, in a sort of paradise of silence.'"

"And then," Katina continued, "the effects of the water nearly killed her. She was so ill, and her brain had been so badly treated, that she begged them not to try again. She promised that she was cured and would be a perfect State student, pretending that the operation had been a success. She proposed a new role as a sort of ambassador, encouraging other students.

Of course she felt bad about that, but this a matter of survival. Not just for herself. She knew that you were a part of something very important, and she knew that you would return. It seemed vital to her that she stayed alive and well."

I exhaled and said, "So you worked out this little plan within the plan."

"Yes. She played her part very well."

"I, we, owe her so much. I want to thank her."

"Do so. She's come to say goodbye."

I spun round. She was standing under one of the trees. She smiled shyly.

"Thank you, Elika. I hope you won't be in trouble."

"I might be. That doesn't matter. You are the important one."

I heard the faint hum as the Professor approached on his little flying machine.

I said, "A last hug, please, Elika."

She came forward and we embraced as the Professor touched down beside us. I pushed her across the Professor's knees, holding her down, and shouted, "Go!"

He looked startled, angry, bewildered. But he never stayed for more than a few seconds. The machine rose. He snapped, "You. . . ." I didn't hear what came after that as he and Elika rose swiftly into the cold night air.

"Oh, Lanny," Katina groaned.

CHAPTER TWENTY-TWO

"*Why?*"

Katina was darting about, in a very humanlike agitated twitch.

I sighed. "It seemed the right thing to do."

"And how much thinking did you put into that?"

"Oh, about a quarter of a second."

"The plan, Lanny! The Programme!"

"The plan to recruit the right people? The plan to replace callousness with compassion, cruelty with kindness, indifference with consideration?"

"In the agreed way, Lanny. No improvising."

"Improvising has been essential because we can plan only so far. It's just that this improvisation was clearly not in accordance with what was agreed."

"So, it was the wrong thing to do."

"Yes. But you now have another valuable asset on the mountain."

"And in danger of losing the most valuable one down here."

"The Professor could come back for me, when he's calmed down."

"He *could*, but a double rescue is going against the way that we agreed to do it. Do you really think that you and Elika can go from the fourteenth floor of a hospital to complete disappearance without some connections being made?"

I sat down. The alley in which we were hiding wasn't the best place for sitting, but I was still weak, and trying to think my way through thick knots always made me tired.

I said, "Then I must go back."

"And have the Final Step?"

"No. You see, I was drugged and kidnapped, then dumped in that filthy river, which is going to make me so ill, that the operation must be deferred."

"That might mean your being so ill that you die."

"Well, yes, there is that. And there is the opposite possibility that in trying to become ill, I shan't."

"At least you're providing your own obstacles."

"I need an emergency hiding place. A place in which to disappear. And we need a communication system. We can't rely on chats under trees. If I'm allowed out, I'll be watched very closely."

"Lanny, you seem to be forgetting that being very ill will defer the operation for a few days, weeks at the most; as soon as you are fit enough to walk, they'll do it. You won't be allowed out until you have been altered."

I continued to think. "In that case, I shall have to convince them that I have not recovered; at least not in that part of me on which they want to operate."

I looked at her, hovering in the moonlight, like a moth that couldn't decide which way to go. She was silent for several minutes, and I knew that a discussion was taking place.

"You need to move quickly. I don't like any part of it, but if you're going to do it, you must hurry."

"Yes. Katina, we'll have to manage without meeting places or hiding places. I'll be on my own. If I fail, you have two excellent new recruits to carry on the good work. Goodbye."

I ran away from her, not looking back, not looking up. But

running was silly. I couldn't outpace her, and I could draw attention to myself. I slowed down, and moved closer to the buildings, trying to walk quietly. I didn't see any OGs, but I saw an occasional disc floating about. Each time, I stopped and stood absolutely still. They could still detect the heat of my body, but I didn't know what their effective distances were. Besides, there was nothing else I could do.

Whether fate was for me or against me, I couldn't say: it depended on whether or not my reaching the river without being accosted was a good thing or a bad thing. Standing on the bank, I didn't feel at all brave and reckless, as I had earlier. I didn't like being ill. In that respect, the State's anti-all pills suited me very well. And now I was going to plunge into the thick sliminess of typhoid, cholera, whatever diseases that slow, brown water was carrying. And not just plunge, but swallow some.

It was top diving board time again. That really was useful training. If it must be done, then do it. I stepped out and dropped into the water. I didn't need to drink any: the shock of the stink as I broke the scummy surface made me gasp, and in went the water, making me choke, making me flounder, thinking that I was going to drown in seconds. The horror of this stinking morass had made me lose my ability to think clearly, thrusting me into a dark hole of terror and panic.

My feet touched the soft mud beneath, giving me the confidence to bob in what I hoped was the direction of the bank. I arrived in seconds, and felt ashamed as I remembered that I had stepped in from the bank, and the water wasn't flowing, so I could hardly have gone far from safety.

How could such a trembling lump of cowardice hope to go through what lay ahead, in which courage and sharp wits were essential? I dragged myself out of the water, feeling the chill now, feeling nauseous, feeling weak and frightened. I didn't want to be ill, and I didn't want to fight the State. I wanted to be given some medicine to make me well, put in a warm bed, then settle down to a calm life of obedience, beans and rice.

Why fight it? Why resist? You only lose in the end.

"What are you doing?" The metallic voice cut through the darkness, the stench, and my fears. I felt a small glow of elation. Yes, I wanted those things, all of them, because I needed safety while I planned and prepared.

"Help," I called weakly, and I collapsed.

"I said what are you doing?"

"Don't know," I mumbled. "What happened?"

I could hear the callous idiot calling for assistance. Good. The more the merrier. You've a big hospital just behind you, idiot, so try making the connection. I could hear a lot of buzzing and crackling, and he kept making jerky little responses which weren't quite words because people at the other end weren't giving him time to speak. Good. It was all good. Let's have lots of excitement, and a big audience for my performance.

"Don't move," said the idiot.

I gave him a look of incredulity, and vomited on his boots.

I wasn't surprised that different types and different levels were taking a keen interest in me. And I wasn't surprised that I was receiving both brutal and tender treatment as they tried to make me well while displaying their anger and resentment.

"Tell me again," said the security officer beside my bed. "You were on the fourteenth floor, and you flew out of the window, and fell into the river. Is that it?"

I hadn't said that or anything like it. He was applying an interrogation technique. There were so many sarcastically withering responses in my brain, but they had to stay there. I must stay in character. I was playing the role of someone who was, temporarily at least, mentally deranged.

I showed him my trying to think face, lots of frowns, wrinkled forehead, silently moving lips. "No," I said, looking puzzled about it. "No. I can't *fly*. How could I *fly*? I was . . . people . . .

blanket . . . needle . . . not the river!" I opened my eyes as wide as I could, forced my mouth into a silent snarl, and curled my fingers into claws. Then, I started to slash, close to his face, making him move back in alarm. "NOT THE RIVER!" I shouted. "NO! NOT THE RIVER!"

I collapsed into my blankets, sobbing. Minutes later, they were injecting me with sedative. That was nice. With feigned agitation, sedation was going to send me off into a deep sleep. And if they decided to wake me in the middle of that, I'd not even need to act the part of someone who was mentally deranged.

<hr />

"You see," said Citizen Security Officer 1, "your story is so preposterous that we'd be failing in our duty as security officers if we believed it."

He was standing by the window, talking in a quiet pleasant way, beginning with my room, my treatment, the weather, and then, as though it were all part of the same thing, he told me that they didn't believe me.

I looked at him as he looked at me, and I gave him a sad smile. No protestations, no insistences, no frustration. Mental derangement of the serene kind.

He said, "Windows shouldn't be open up here. People could be tempted to . . . I'll arrange for a lock to be put on it."

Bad news. I looked straight ahead.

"As soon as you're well enough, we'll torture it out of you."

I waved a weak arm at him, indicating that I wanted him to come closer. Much closer. He leaned forward.

I whispered, "Bedpan."

CHAPTER TWENTY-THREE

HIS FULL TITLE was Citizen Security Officer 1 Stern. That last one was his name, not a description. He was close to being my constant companion. Urbane is the word. Because of this, he was the most sinister and frightening interrogation officer of all. With each day, I was recovering, and with each day, he talked about my imminent full recovery, and my ensuing torture. He said it as someone might encourage a patient's recovery by talking about the flowers and the trees.

I was glad that the medical people liked to give me sedatives. Occasionally, I had to renew the supply, as it were, with a little private show of hysteria. The main thing was to be torpid and docile for the master interrogators. When they let me.

"Why . . . why . . . torture?" I murmured. "W . . . what've I done?"

"A lot of things, Citizen Student Javid Yong. You are a traitor."

"Javid Yong," I said. "That's me. Not traitor. No. Good boy. Always good boy." I started to cry. I could make the tears flow now because I was still weak, and I *was* very sad.

"No," Javid," he said, coming closer, but not bedpan request close. "No, not good boy. Very bad boy."

"What'd I do?" *Yes, what did I do? Not suspicions, but actual, proved offences.*

"A lot of things, Citizen Student. Oh, you were very clever about it. But we're not stupid. We watched you closely, and you kept making mistakes."

As he was talking, my eyes were moving round the room, showing my failure to concentrate. When he finished, I waited for a few seconds, then looked at him again, and said, "You're not a doctor."

"Stop it!"

I began to flap my arms at him. "Go away! Leave me alone! I won't go! NOT THE RIVER! PLEASE, NOT THE RIVER!"

Through my sobbing, I heard his grunt of frustration.

Just another actor.

With the brisk efficiency that the State could summon when it suited it, a locksmith came and quickly fastened the window with a lock. Now, I was completely trapped. I decided to have a stroll. Part of the act, and a bit of reconnoitring. And a bit of exercise. The thought made me a bit cheery, and I had to force that down. Bewildered, always bewildered. That was how I must stay.

Sliding out of bed and standing made me feel like an invalid. No acting required. I eased the door open, intending to peep out, but decided that a genuinely bewildered person wouldn't do that. I set off along the corridor, with a softly plodding walk, looking around me.

The reconnoitring part of it didn't happen because coming along the corridor were a doctor and Citizen Security Officer 1.

"No!" the doctor called, in a doctorly way of disapproving.

"Where do you think you're going?" was the predictable response of my interrogator.

I paused and blinked. "Home," I said. I looked around with

my mouth open. "I don't like this place. Too much evil. It *smells* of evil. I'm going home."

I started to hurry past them.

"No. you aren't!" Citizen Security Officer 1 sounded annoyed.

The doctor grabbed an arm and said, "Come on back to your room. You aren't well enough to go home yet."

Or to have the Final Step. Keep it up, doctor. I'll come quietly. No resistance from me. As we walked along, I babbled, "Is anyone coming for tea tonight? Is it beans and rice or rice and beans?" My little private joke, which seemed to fit the current situation.

When I was back in bed, I was given another sedative, and almost smiled at the Stern man and his attempts to trip me. He went straight into his routine.

"This story of yours, this fantasy about being kidnapped and dumped in the river. . . . "

I whimpered, "Not the river. Please not the river."

He tried to be patient. "No. No. You were *in* the river. We found you in the river."

"*In* the river? Was I swimming?"

Still trying to be patient. "No. You had climbed out of the . . . why am I explaining? It's *your* fantasy. You *know* what happened. It's no good, Yong. You might fool the doctors, but you aren't fooling me."

I had widened my eyes as he snapped at me, the smooth manner lying in a crumpled heap like a discarded costume. "Why are you shouting at me? You're too noisy. I want to go home."

He strode over to the bed and shouted, "How did you do it? Eh? How did you go from the fourteenth floor to the river?"

"The *river*?" I said it with a quavering voice.

"No, don't start that again. Forget. Just tell me how you went from all the way up here to all the way down there. From the top floor, all the way down to the ground."

He almost sang the last bit, in his incredulous, and very sarcastic, tone.

"Who did?"

"YOU DID!" He grabbed the neck of my gown and shook me.

It was only in that moment that the truth of this struck me: all this wasn't entirely about me as a person, or even as a minor menial in the system: this was about his, and their, fear. There were only two possible explanations for my escape: either I was kidnapped or otherwise removed, or I went all that way on my own. The only other possibility was an impossibility. Looking out of the window on that first day wasn't just a part of his casual act: he was looking for drainpipes, indentations for gripping, ivy, nearby trees.

Something was happening, and the State didn't understand it, and couldn't control it. At least, it felt endangered. Either I acted alone in a superhuman way, or I had assistance, voluntary or otherwise, which meant people working against the State; people who didn't want me to be interrogated, who wanted me to be drowned or poisoned in that filthy river.

A rebellion.

Well-organised, because this was the fourteenth floor.

Were hospital workers involved?

Was the Outer Guardian who found me involved?

As he shook me, I wanted to laugh at him.

It was time to increase my performance. I yelped, cried out, pushed him away, slithered across the bed, and fell out. I staggered across the room, wailing in a barely human way. He cut across and grabbed me. "Shut up, you little faker. Back to bed!"

I bellowed, "Help! Murder! HELP ME! HE'S GOING TO PUT ME IN THE RIVER!"

I thought the mention of the river was a nice touch of obsessive dread.

The door opened, and a nurse stood staring. All she said was, "Um." Then she hurried away.

He sneered. "No help there."

In other circumstances, this man would have been a simple torturing, murdering sadist. But the State had provided career opportunities for such people.

I decided on a change of pace and volume. I whimpered, "Just kill me," and sagged as though I had died.

I heard the swish as the door opened again.

"Help me to put him back in bed."

The doctor remembered that he was a doctor and forgot that he was in the presence of a Citizen Security Officer 1. "Why was he out of bed?"

"I don't know." What a feeble response.

"He tried to kill me," I said to the doctor as he lay me back in the bed. "Don't leave me alone with him. He said he'll put me back in the river."

I said it with rapidly growing anxiety, trying to clutch the doctor's arms. I was pleased to hear him say quietly, as though to himself, "He had a sedative. I don't know what could have excited him. I'll give him another one. And, er, you'd better leave him for a while."

I gave the doctor a look of deep gratitude, and the other, a look of fear and horror.

The doctor escorted him out, and moments later, I was given another sedative. I hoped that now I could be left in peace to let both sedatives have their full effect.

All this acting was very tiring.

CHAPTER TWENTY-FOUR

When the nurse came in with a bit of breakfast, I gripped her with one arm, and pointed with the other. "They keep coming into my room," I gasped in a hoarse voice.

"Who do?" she asked, wanting to leave the food and go.

"Rats. Hundreds of them. They come down at night. From there."

She looked to where I was pointing. "That's just the old loft hatch. Under the roof. It's a very old building. There's nothing there. Don't you think people would have seen any rats about."

"Nothing up there?"

"No, unless people have been dumping."

I didn't persist. I didn't want her to go telling people that I was having hallucinations concerning the loft hatch. I just wanted to know what it was.

Was there a way out of there, and a way down?

When Citizen Security Officer Stern appeared, he said, "What's all this about rats?"

I looked at him as though I was trying to work things out. I said softly, "What happened to me? Am I in hospital?"

I couldn't see any other way of diverting him away from the loft hatch. If I continued my act, how could I change the subject? He'd persist about the rats, and how they came into the room.

He looked grimly pleased. "You had a bad fall, Javid. You fell in the river. Don't you remember?"

"The river," I said, starting to sound anxious again. "What was I . . . why . . . ?"

"Don't you remember anything?"

I put my hands over my eyes, then took them away and stared about the room. "People . . . darkness . . . trapped . . . struggling to breathe . . . whispering. . . ." I looked at him. "W-what have you done to me? Have you been torturing me? I remember torture. Ice cold, then burning. I remember that! What have you done?"

I was crawling out of the bed, my face contorted in mad rage. I snarled and hissed. He walked quickly to the door, and called for a nurse. When one appeared, he said, "Sedative. Quickly. Double dose."

I dropped to my knees and screwed myself into a ball, muttering, "What have you done to me?"

I stayed like that while the needle was stuck in me again, and then I let them put me back in the bed. I was pleased with my performance, switching from plain old madness to a sort of amnesiac nervous breakdown, and putting the blame on them for the torture. I thought it added some realism to my other pretence, and kept him distracted, and away from direct action.

I turned my face to the pillow, mumbling, "What did they do to you. Javvy? Tortured you. That's what. Ice cold, burned, then threw you in the river. State wants to kill you."

"No, Citizen Student," came the quiet voice behind me. "Not at all. You don't know what you're saying. You are ill. The State wants you to be well. The State is taking good care of you. And tomorrow, you will go from here, and the State will make you perfectly well."

I made some incomprehensible noises into the pillow, did a

little sigh, and pretended to go to sleep. And as I heard the door shut, I did sleep.

———

Was I dreaming? I had left my bed and walked to the big window. It was night, and the city glittered in the darkness. Nothing but a shattered tinsel bauble. A gathering of idiots wallowing in a pit of ignorance and self-delusion. What satisfaction was there for the State in having absolute control over billions of people who no longer thought, no longer cared?

Was I dreaming? Were we all dreaming? What was the point of it all, if there was no hope?

But there *was* hope! In my pretence of madness, I had seen Citizen Security Officer Stern, representative of the State, perplexed, doubting, *worried*. Never forget that. I was here, and then I was there, and he can't work out how it happened, and he's bothered, *they* are bothered, because that is a crack in the wall, and unless it's repaired, it will grow.

Hope, Katina! I have seen it. I have made it. I have received it.

I willed her to come to me.

And there she was, hovering so close, but outside that locked window. For a few moments, we seemed to exchange telepathic messages, as I told her not to break the glass because that would tell them that a disc had done it. I pointed upwards, and she understood.

Quickly now. I stood on a chair, and pressed the hatch. It clicked and dropped open. No time for being weak, no hesitation. I gripped as well as I could, let my legs swing forward, then pulled myself up and over. I reached down and pulled the hatch shut. That was good so far, but I was now in complete blackness.

As my eyes adjusted, I thought I saw a faint smudge of grey, which might be a window. I felt my way across a big mess of discarded items, metal, plastic, cardboard. I kept stumbling, and became aware that I was making noises which could be heard in the room below.

I froze in terror as I heard voices. No, please not now. I heard the voice of Stern calling, "Javid! We know you're up there. You can't escape. Come down now!"

I could keep still or continue towards what I hoped was a skylight, making revealing noises all the way. The decision was made for me, from below and above. I heard the hatch click open behind me, and I saw a a darker patch against the patch of grey in the roof. Stern was coming. Katina was waiting!

"Javid! I can see you. Come down immediately!"

Katina was waiting. Katina could be seen. Stern's head showed in the light from the room. I gripped something metallic, a broken chair or table, and hurled it towards him. There was a clump, an exclamation, and a louder clump below. Taking big steps, pushing aside any obstacles, I scrambled over to the skylight. The heap of debris was now in my favour as I stretched up, and found an old latch. The window creaked open very stiffly. There wasn't room for me to fit through. I heard Stern, again, snarling with fury as he thrust himself up through the hatch. I hit the frame of the window with my flat hand, and it creaked a little more open. It would have to be enough. Stern was already struggling across the mess.

I gripped and pulled. Something sharp stuck in my back. Ignore it! Pull, squirm, push. A hand touched my left foot, and my right foot responded with a kick to his head. But the effort made me sink back down. But this time, with one big pull, I soared through the narrow gap onto the roof tiles. I pushed the window down, every second being vital, and followed Katina precariously along the sloping roof.

"Now!"

I didn't hesitate. I gripped, and leapt off the roof.

As always, our flight was in a long downward curve. Below, I could see the flashing lights of security cars, summoned to the hospital for this one person, this anomaly.

This crack in the wall.

We landed on a flat roof. Katina said, "It wasn't safe to wait in a park again. The Professor has been on the alert. He won't be long." After a short pause, she said, "You can let go of me now."

"I don't want to," I replied.

I could still see the flashing lights and hear the sirens as the Professor arrived, in his quiet way.

"No surprises this time, I hope," he said.

"No, Professor. I just want to go home. And before I resume training, I want a short rest."

"And a change of clothes. In that hospital gown, you're going to find it extremely chilly."

I remembered, and groaned.

CHAPTER TWENTY-FIVE

So, the one became three. I was rather pleased with myself.

"It should have been two," the Professor growled. "That was a complete breakdown in discipline. Three people have disappeared, one of them a model student, a keen recruiter for Final Step volunteers." He shook his head. "You and Mikel were relatively insignificant people. Removing Elika was a big mistake. It . . . it was emotional. It was going against the Plan, against my instructions, against all your training and preparation."

I stopped feeling pleased with myself.

The Professor was pacing about, angry and thoroughly vexed. With me. "The *Plan*, Lanny. We agreed it was the Plan above everything else. Above all relationships, all emotional ties, above family. And . . . and you go down there, making eyes, yes, you did, at Elika, at your father . . . putting the whole thing in jeopardy. It's not good enough, Lanny."

"Elika approached me. She was involved in my escape."

"And that one was Katina's fault. Finding Elika, like finding an orphan and taking pity on her, then dragging her into the plot. And Elika was stupid to become involved. And you were stupid to let her become involved, and . . . puh, what a gang of emotionally unstable idiots instead of the calm, rational builders of the future that I envisaged."

"What do you expect, Professor? You're recruiting from a corrupt world in which the act of thinking is suppressed, in which absolute conformity is mandatory, in which *everyone* is a spy on everyone else. Do you want to surround yourself with scientists up here on the mountain? Well, the bad news is that the scientists were absorbed and controlled by the State long ago. So were the supposed intellectuals, the politicians, the writers, the philosophers, the creators. In fact, all those were the first to go. They were the most capable at rationalising their failure to be rational. The State uses false logic all the time. Everything is explained and justified. And those who disagree are mentally defective. Well, they must be because false logic demands it."

"And what are you doing?" He was still stamping about. "*You're* rationalising *your* failure to be rational. If all the supposed thinkers have been captured and brainwashed, it's up to you to do the thinking. That is the essence of the Plan."

"I wasn't saying that I haven't failed: I was explaining why I failed, and why I shall always fail. I'm still a young person, sent back to attend school. I recruited other schoolchildren. What was I supposed to do? Bring back a few teachers?"

He stopped pacing, and stared at Mikel and Elika, already reading a couple of his history books.

I said, "I wanted to be what you wanted me to be. I tried so hard. Then, things kept happening, and I suppose proactivity changed to reactivity."

He was still standing there, staring, thinking.

I said, "I need to boost myself a bit. I'm the equivalent of an only child who's suddenly had a brother and a sister thrust into his cosy little world. I'm now a team member."

He seemed to wake from his thinking. He turned and said, "You did well, Lanny. Of course you did. You and Katina. And the new recruits did, in their different ways. And if you're no longer an only child, think of the reduction in pressure on you.

It won't always be you that has to go back. And, perhaps just a daydream, but I keep thinking of the possibility of sending all three of you down, for maximum recruiting potential."

I shook my head. "Never more than two, until we have more. We must always keep at least one up here. Down there is very dangerous."

"Quite right," said the Professor. "No more daydreaming for me."

"But as we increase, we shall send more down."

"Yes, indeed." He smiled, then frowned. "It is a sad irony that in order to challenge that system, we are employing the same methods that they used in the beginning. An agent here, an agent there, a whisper here, a murmur there."

"The difference is that we aren't trying to impose a system: we really are just rescuing people from that system. We can't replace it with anything, not until our new society up here has grown, and is ready to do the replacing."

"Yes, we must be patient. But I hope that we shan't be too late. Even if all the billions were released from tyranny, would they know what to do? How do switched-off brains start to function again?"

I held my arm out towards Mikel and Elika. "It can be done."

"Yes," he said. "You and they are the future."

"We have the minds, and the enthusiasm, and we depend on you to teach us. Would you really want scientists and intellectuals up here? Within minutes, they'd be aguing about how we should do things, and setting up groups, committees and political parties."

"Lectured to by my pupil!"

"Only reminding you of what you already know."

He smiled. "Keep reminding me, Lanny."

I glanced round. He said, "She's nearby. She never goes far from you. She'll help the others, too, of course. But a good dog is friendly to all, loyal to one."

"So, if she goes down there with Mikel or Elika, it will be strictly business."

"Yes. I think I'd put it like that."

Katina floated over. "Lanny will tell you that I was frequently very sharp with him, to keep him from distractions and deviations."

"Yes, Katina. I was weak, and I needed you to be firm with me."

The Professor looked serious again. "Only a short rest for you, Lanny. It's all preparation. I need you back in training. You've been slouching about in that other society, you've been in a filthy river, then treated with what I daren't imagine in the hospital, and you've had a considerable amount of stress. I think you need a month of strict training before we even start to think about who and what you will be for your next visit."

"Visit? Mission, please."

"Hopefully, next time, it will be much more . . . enjoyable." He rose to his feet. "Well, I think I shall go and make a bit of lunch for us all."

As he walked away, I said, "Ah. Decent food again. What are you planning, Professor?"

He called over his shoulder, "I thought we'd have some beans and rice."

I looked at Katina. "He's joking, isn't he? Tell me he's joking."

"Who knows?" was her only reply.

"Of course he's joking," I said, setting off after him, just in case.

THE END.

ABOUT THE AUTHOR

John Guthrie writes speculative fiction for all ages, from children to adults. His books are often set in troubled worlds, whether here on earth or in far-flung planets in other solar systems. At the heart of his books are characters happy with their quiet lives who are ensnared in situations they're desperate to escape from. They don't know whom to trust because trusting the wrong person often leads to the worst possible outcome. You'll find yourself cheering for each of the main characters in John's books as they match wits with the most ruthless of adversaries.

John resides in the UK and, when he's not on the lookout for a stray dog to show up on his doorstep, is continually dreaming up new stories and characters.

If you enjoyed this story, please consider leaving a review at your favorite book site.

Follow John on Facebook at tinyurl.com/5n82ch69, and for a full list of his books, visit www.john-guthrie-author.com.

f

* 9 7 8 1 0 6 8 4 6 1 2 0 0 *